I knew I had to kill Seema. It had to be done. There was no other way.

Maybe you never think of murder till you are pushed to the brink. I had been pushed...

All that money. When she died.

If she died. Seema was as strong as a cow...

I had not stopped working in the past twenty years. College and Law school had depleted me. I had drudged to be a top student. The past fifteen years of law practice had changed me. All ideals learnt at the school had been beaten out of me...

The courts were places of lawlessness. Procedures were gimmicked. Witnesses prevented from giving facts and tricked into admitting half-truths and untruths. It was a racket. And the prize went to the smartest racketeer.

I wanted money. All of it.

I had to be smarter than police detectives like Govinda Raju and his tribe — some of them who had been lawyers and were reputedly clever.

It was a challenge that was worthy of me.
My life staked against Seema's money —
and my freedom!

PERFECT MURDER

SHAKUNTALA DEVI

Print ISBN: 978-81-222-0706-4
eISBN: 978-81-222-0541-1

Perfect Murder

1st Published 1976
This Printing 2023

Published by:
Orient Paperbacks
(A division of Vision Books Pvt. Ltd.)
5A/8 Ansari Road, 1st Floor
Daryaganj, New Delhi — 110002
www.orientpaperbacks.in

Printed and bound at TACT Print.

To

Inspector Govinda Raju

PERFECT MURDER

I KNEW I had to kill Seema. It had to be done. There was no other way. Maybe you never think of murder till you are pushed to the brink. I had been pushed.

All that money. About fifty lakhs. All mine when she died. If she died. Seema was strong as a cow; she was going to live for ever, hoarding every rupee. Forever denying me anything of which she disapproved — and she had been reared to disapprove of anything related to frivolous pleasure and vanity. The way she doled out money to me was insulting, and when she gave a hundred rupees to throw away, she beamed as if she were a Lady Bountiful.

I had not stopped working for a minute in the past twenty years. College and Law School had depleted me. I had stayed in the upper third of my class, but I drudged. Maybe even in the fifteen years of practice I had begun looking at things in a slanted, cock-eyed way. All the ideals learnt at school were quickly beaten out of me, and I fought back with every trick I knew.

I saw innocent men convicted and criminals escape

justice. I had begun thinking I represented forces of law and order. I found that courts were places of lawlessness, where intelligent jurors were not wanted, where procedure was so gimmicked that witnesses were prevented from giving important facts and tricked into admitting half-truths, untruths. It had become a racket to me. And the prize went to the smartest racketeer. I wanted something else — freedom... and fifty lakhs of rupees. To get it I had to be smarter than police detectives like Govinda Raju and CID cops — men who once had been lawyers and were reputedly clever.

It was a challenge that I felt was worthy of me. My life staked against Seema's money — and my freedom!

THE THREE OF them sat in my office, glancing at one another. My secretary came in and I had them run through the story again, but Pushpa's taking notes unnerved them and they were already changing what they had told me.

I leaned back and studied them. The old woman appeared about 60, and her sister might be around 55. She fidgeted with her fingers and kept patting Mrs Khanna's hand, but otherwise added nothing. The younger sister's husband, sprawled in a leather chair, was the real doll. He was the man with all the answers — and the only one of the two who had witnessed the tragedy.

Suddenly I felt tired. I had had enough for one night. I called a halt. I told them to return the following evening at six and in the meantime to sort out the angles, so we could get together a coherent brief. I reminded myself that murder was a serious business and they would never keep

Mrs Khanna's son away from the gallows by contradicting one another.

Pushpa showed them out. I glanced at my wrist watch, feeling depleted in a way that had nothing to do with them.

I stared at Pushpa. She was standing rigidly, her face flushed, and she said something.

'What?' I said.

'It's late. After nine. Is that all, Mr Sharma?'

Her blue nylon sari had faint pink threads in it. Her sleeveless blouse had a plunging neckline. I remembered I had hired her because, at first glance, I had decided she was a very charming girl to have around the office. That was one year ago. After she had been with me a while, I began to feel things for her. And I began to see she was very attractive, and so different, not like any other woman at all!

First thing that got inside me was when I saw she wasn't just what she was pretending to be. Even at ten to five she was cool, sedate and efficient. I got to wondering what she did away from the office. Where did she go for amusement? What music did she enjoy? Did she dance? Did she drink? And sometimes her dark brown eyes had flecks in them, fear or old hurts, secretive and hidden. I shrugged it off. So Pushpa was not the simple, uncomplex soul she appeared to be. It was not my affair. She knew what I wanted in a secretary, and played the part expertly.

'Sure. That's all,' I said. 'Thanks, Pushpa.'

'They are odd, aren't they?' she frowned, 'You can't tell what to believe.'

I shrugged. 'You haven't been in this racket very long. You'll believe what they want you to believe. You'll keep going over it with them till they believe it themselves. Finally, you'll take it to a court and try to make the judge believe it.'

'They seemed so nervous, especially the man.'

I smiled wryly. 'A dangerous character. A no-good who wants to feel important. I'll get a deposition from him and drop him out of the case. I couldn't afford to have him on my side.'

'You really think you can save her son from the gallows?'

'If I didn't, I wouldn't have taken the case.'

I watched her walk towards the door. I watched her slim straight back, the long lustrous hair braided and falling to her waist. She paused, hand on the knob. That silhouette could keep you awake at nights.

'I know you are tired, Mr Sharma —'

'No, what's wrong?'

She hesitated. 'I want to ask a favour — and I hate to —'

'Why should you? One year and you haven't asked a favour. You've caught me in an expansive mood. What's troubling you?' I nodded towards a chair. She sat down and crossed her legs, gripping the shorthand pad and pencil tightly in her lap.

'It's — this girl friend of mine, Mr Sharma. Her husband — well, he got into trouble, embezzling from his firm — and was sent to prison for two years. He has served more than half of his term and is eligible for parole, but needs help — from a good lawyer.'

'Ask your friend to come in, and see me.'

She bit her lip. 'She — might not have much money.'

'That's all right Pushpa. For a friend of yours we can work out something.'

She stirred in her chair. 'No. I mean — if it's all right with you — she's had so much trouble and expense and all — I would rather keep this — about the money — between you and me.'

I should have frowned. Inside I was frowning, money and lack of it should be on the table between lawyer and clients. 'We can work that out too.'

She went on sitting there for some moments, as though she wanted to say more. I grew silent in the office, silent in the quiet building, as if waiting for something.

Bangalore was an overgrown city, but no metropolis, and in Bangalore I was well known. I drove home slowly, telling myself to get her out of my mind. The farther Seema and I drifted apart, the more I thought of Pushpa. First I told myself I was too smart to get into a love affair. I wanted her. It was that simple. I could have her for a weekend somewhere — at Jog Falls or Brindavan Gardens, or for that matter even in Ooty or Kodaikanal, if I could arrange it and never think of her again. Or I could be really smart and give her the sack after that.

But I didn't like the very thought of dismissing her. I did not like to think about that office without her in it. I did not suggest a weekend somewhere either. At home I was wound tighter and tighter. Seema started talking about how I was working too hard, having too much on my mind, and how I needed to see a doctor. Finally she had made an appointment with Dr Jagannath, but I laughed at that, I did not need a doctor to tell me what the matter was with me. I did not believe any doctor could explain why I could not get Pushpa out of my mind even when I wanted to. But just the same I could not do it. The days went by. The situation became worse — much worse.

I turned off Bellary Road and into the side road, and when I reached my driveway, I wondered really how I had got there. This house in palace orchards had cost Seema five lakhs of rupees. And a couple of lakhs more had gone into extras — landscaping, interior decoration, and the swimming pool that remained empty and leaf-pocked most of the time.

I parked in the car park and went through the sun parlour entrance, carrying my briefcase. Seema was doing her intricate knitting in the front room. I started towards the staircase leading to the bedroom.

'Kamal?'

'Yes, Seema.'

'Where have, you been?'

I dropped my briefcase in the lobby and leaned, on the doorjamb. 'Where have I been? Haven't some of your well-intentioned friends reported to you yet?'

'Don't be vicious, Kamal. It's after ten. I just asked. Shouldn't I be interested in you? What else do I have to be interested in?'

'God knows. I don't have the secret information service you do.'

'You are in a foul mood. Why, Kamal? I am the one who should be. I had dinner alone. Then I went to the Sarkar's and played bridge. What could I tell them? — That I never see you. That I live my solitary existence, and you have your life, your work, your friends, all the things you'd rather do than come home.'

'I had to work late.'

'I don't believe you.'

'I don't care.'

'Of course you don't care. Why should Kamalakar Sharma, Barrister-at-Law, the distinguished lawyer, care what his wife thinks. I phoned your office twice in the evening. I got no answer.'

'Seema, I left my office just fifteen minutes back!'

'I've my doubts.'

'Lord, Seema, if I were as rich as you, I wouldn't work

late. I'd come home straight and watch you knit.'

'Is there something else you'd rather I did. Maybe you would like it better if I ran around. I could, you know.'

'Why not? Go ahead and try.'

'That would be sweet wouldn't it? Maybe you don't care what people think about you. But I do.'

'Seema, I was just going to have a drink. Will you have one with me?'

'You always think I'm so happy because father left me money. Father wanted me to have the things I wanted. What do I have? A husband too busy for me, too wrapped up in himself —'

'You want a Martini or Coca-Cola?'

'I hate alcohol, and you know it.'

I walked past her, and opened the portable bar. I mixed a Martini five to one. I opened a bottle of Coca-Cola, poured it in a glass and handed it to her. I carried my glass and sat down beside her.

'I want to have interests too, Kamal. But you are not interested. You want that office. I could give you anything.'

Sure. Anything except money. Her father had willed her fifty lakhs he had accumulated like a squirrel. Sinful to spend, sinful to waste. sinful to throw it away on pleasure. Hoard it. Stack it up. And Seema inherited all his traits along with the money.

'I want money of my own. Unfortunately, I know no way to get it except by working.'

'I wouldn't mind your working — but I hate the way you run around with women.'

'Would it make you happier if I ran around with men?'

'Don't be silly. You know what I mean. My friends see you. And they talk about it. I feel embarrassed.'

I ran my eyes over her. I noticed she was heavy, steadily

getting heavier. I was in my mid-forties. She was a few years younger. She still looked very pretty. Her auburn hair was neatly cut and smoothly set.

You've got yourself a wonderful existence, Kamalakar Sharma, I told myself. Wonderful. Everything a man could want. My trouble was I coveted nice things. My income was rising — but in this profession it takes time — to make big money. Time I hated wasting when Seema was loaded with the stuff, and didn't even understand how to enjoy it. I put my arm round her.

'Do I give you a bad time, Seema?'

'You don't make it easy.'

'Come taste my drink.'

'I don't want to taste your drink. I don't have to get drunk to enjoy myself.'

I pulled her closer. She leaned towards me awkwardly. 'Let's go to bed, Seema.'

She didn't even know what I was talking about. 'Not yet Kamal. I want to finish this line. If I stop, these stitches won't be right.'

I sighed, finished my drink, got up and poured another.

'Kamal, you are not going to get so drunk. You can't make it to bed, can you?'

'God forbid.' I finished off the second Martini looking at Seema. Poor little rich girl, with all that money. Fifty lakhs! When I started from the room, she wanted to know where I was going. I remembered to be polite. I had cost her a lot of money getting where I was. And where was I?

I had met Seema during my first year at college. And I do not know how it happened or why it happened. But we fell in love. At least at that time I thought it was love. There was a big gap between us socially. She was the only daughter of a leading industrialist, heiress to a great fortune. I was a struggling student, barely able to pay my tuition fee. Son of a schoolmaster.

Seema wanted me. And her father wanted Seema to have the best. He always wanted everything best for his daughter. I am not certain whether or not I liked it at that time. But he underwrote the rest of my college career and then the Law School in England. He said my law schooling was the best investment he could ever make for Seema.

I married Seema before I went to England to join the law school. I do not know exactly when it happened. But almost a few days after the marriage, I realized that I did not love Seema. I did not hate her. Just that I had no feelings for her at all!

Her father died immediately on my return to India, and Seema came into the money!

I flopped across the bed, thinking here was the end of another gracious evening at home with the Kamalakar Sharma's. I wondered if Seema ever guessed how much I wanted her to die!

THE NEXT MORNING I awoke in the same sour mood. The man awaiting me at my office did not help to brighten my day.

Govinda Raju, a detective inspector — a policeman. That is all there is to say about him. You can describe him, say where he lives and what he eats and what he wears, but when you have referred to him as a 'policeman', you have said it all. It was his whole life. He told me what it was like being a policeman. I believed him. Let any man step out of the line and he has got the belt coming to him. Govinda Raju was the man to apply the belt.

'When a man pulls something, I owe him no consideration. Nothing. He steps out on his wife and gets into trouble. Why should I keep his wife from knowing? He asked for it. Once a man breaks the law, he should expect the consequences. Not just some of them — all of them.'

Some company for me, the way I felt that morning. When I felt better, I kidded Govinda Raju. I told him he would wreck 99 per cent of marriages and full the jails to overflowing if he practised such ideas. He had no sense of humour and he could never take a joke. He would tell me with a serious face. 'We've got laws. That's what we've got them for, to obey. Right?'

I had long since stopped arguing with him. Sometimes I wondered how he had existed 38 years in this complex society with his unrealistic views. But I never asked him. Like most lawyers, I disliked policemen. I disliked Govinda Raju in particular. When he opposed me on a witness stand, he was stubborn. A hard nut to crack. He gave the jury the impression of being right, even when he was wrong.

'In this report on the Khanna case,' I said, 'it shows you investigated the death?'

'That's right.'

'Did you think it looked like self-defence?'

'Ha!... ha!... what a joke!'

'Justifiable homicide?'

'That's a good one. Guys like you make a living off words, don't you. But I've never seen it. Murder is murder. It's a crime. I don't see how it's justifiable in any circumstances.'

'They say the old man beat his wife often. He was cruel to all of them. And he repeatedly threatened the boy.'

'If the boy didn't like things — the way it was going on, he could clear out. Who could have stopped him?'

'What about the old woman?'

'If she didn't like her life with the old man, she could have moved in with her son. No one expected her to be his slave.'

I stared at him.

'Maybe it wasn't so easy. The old man had all the money. The wife had no independent means. And the boy had no job!'

'All right. So they were well and comfortable with the old man. What did they want? A heaven on earth! They knew the old man had a violent temper, liked to rule his house the way his father had ruled it before him —'

'That can be pretty sickening, you know.'

'Not enough to excuse a murder. Listen. That Khanna kid lay in the bed night after night and planned how he was going to kill that old man. Of course I know you've been talking to the brother-in-law. He has got the old woman and the girl all worked up. They think they can get the boy out of jail.'

'You expect to testify for the prosecution?'

'If they ask me.'

'I've got both the sub-inspectors who arrived on the scene.'

He shrugged. 'What do they know? I know the two fellows you're talking about. They know just enough about police work to blow a whistle.'

'Couldn't you ever be wrong, Raju?'

'About murder? No. Never. I've seen too many of them. I've seen all kinds. They all add up to one thing. Murder. Murderers have got a special smell. I can smell them out. You know my record? One case not solved — and I can put my hand on the chap who did that. But he has got an influential family. His uncle is a Minister of something. And

I couldn't get anything but circumstantial evidence against him — evidence that had to be true. I had to let him go. That hurts. It muddles up my record. I won't let it happen again.'

'I've got a good case, Raju. You'll look bad. Mark my word. You'll lose this time. I'm going to beat you this time, Raju.'

He shrugged. 'You won't. No lawyer will, counsellor. If a policeman does his work right, no lawyer can change it.'

'That's where you are wrong. There are always angles,' I said.

'MY FRIEND SAID she would let me know,' Pushpa said when Govinda Raju was gone. She stood beside my desk. Today she wore a pink organdie sari embroidered in white. She looked cool and crisp. She had gathered up her hair into a chignon that rested on the nape of her neck.

'She's so shy. She — she's afraid of you. Mr Sharma, it will take time. She'll have to get up her nerve.'

'She'll get it up if she wants anything done for her husband.'

'Oh yes. She will. It's just that she felt so unhappy. And so afraid of what people will think of her. Because of what her husband did and all. But she needs help. She wants it. She'll let me know.'

I nodded. I tried to concentrate on the briefs on my desk. She went on standing there. After a moment, I looked up. Maybe it was the reflection of the sun through the window. Her face looked flushed.

'I want to thank you. It's fine, what you are doing. I know you're doing it for me.'

'What's a friend for, Pushpa.'

I heard her heavy inhalation. 'I don't know, Mr Sharma. I haven't had very many.'

'Now, you must be joking. A pretty girl like you. No friends!'

'I'm not pretty.'

'All right, you are hideous. No wonder you have no friends. Going around doing things for them — like what you're doing for this friend — what's her name — and her husband?'

'Lata. Oh well, she's different. We went to a commercial institute together. Things troubled her and she had to tell me about them. She shared a room with me — till she got married. I was glad to have her as a friend. I never had one, you know.'

'No, I didn't.'

'Well, my parents died when I was ten. I stayed for a few years with relatives. But they had no room for me in their heart, really. I was a burden. I hate to be a burden on anyone. I always like to pay my own way. Whatever I do. Probably because I was a burden so long.'

I stood up and walked towards her. I touched her shoulder. I could feel the warmth of her against my palm. I kept my voice level. 'You're worried about my fee, Pushpa. Is that it?'

'Partly. I know you'll let me pay you anyway, I can. But I want you to let me pay you.'

There was no sense pretending I did not know what she meant. It was in the way her almond eyes glanced at mine and turned away. She did not move away from the desk. Or away from me. She stood waiting. I looked at her, my pulse pounding heavily. I wanted her.

But I cannot let that happen. We would turn this place

into a love nest. Mornings not opening the front door, evenings working late. Three hours for lunch. I needed something. But not the mess that would result.

I was going to get her out of my mind. And get my mind back to work. All right. My home was not a heaven. But I had my career. I knew what I wanted. This was sticking my hand into a furnace. Reaching for something I really did not even want.

Perhaps I should let her go, and get another girl. But her work was satisfactory. What could I tell her?

I did not believe it. Even when I felt my hand moving on the small of her back, and felt the way she quivered against my hand. Her body moved close against mine. I drew her face up against mine. And I saw her eyes close like a tired baby's. Her lips parted as if she were hungry and thirsty and needing — all the things I was. I was throbbing all over. But for a moment I thought I was wrong — about everything. Her parted mouth was cool against my lips. She held her body rigid.

Her eyes opened and looked straight into mine. For an instant it was as if we hated each other. And then she cried out. And her lips came hard against mine. For a long time I knew only one thing. I wanted her.

'I shouldn't have let you. What will you think of me?'

'I think you're exciting.'

'Yes. But what else? What do you think I am letting you kiss me like that in the office? What if somebody had walked in?'

I did not have my breath back yet. 'You must think I'm cheap,' she said. 'Do you want me to leave?'

'What for?' Some minutes back, I was thinking of getting rid of her. But now I was ready to beg her to stay. 'Why do you want to quit?'

'We can't do this. It's dangerous. We don't know what'll come out of it!'

'I don't care. I know what I want.'

I'd spoil everything for you. I'd be bad for you.'

'Is there somebody else, Pushpa?'

'What?'

'Another man. Someone you love. I know so little about you Pushpa.'

'And I about you.' She shook her head. 'There's nobody else — like this, I mean. Nobody else at all. I know one or two boys. I've dined with them, gone to the movies with them, but nothing — like this.'

'Have they held you, Pushpa? Have they excited you?'

She withdrew herself and walked to the window. 'I never knew a man could make a girl feel the way — the way you make me feel. I knew men got excited. I just never knew a girl was supposed to.'

I gathered her in my arms. 'Good God, you are young.'

She held herself tightly. 'No, that has nothing to do with it.'

'What has?'

'I just never felt this way about anybody else.'

'Thank God, for that.'

'No, it's terrible.'

'Why?'

'I work here. You are my boss — unless you want me to go. I wouldn't blame you, if you want me to.'

'I won't let you get away from me.'

'I — better get back to desk. I've a lot of work.'

'All right.'

'Don't be angry, Mr ... Sharma,' she smiled.

'Now what are you laughing at?'

'If you only knew how I've thought about that — just

how thrilled I have felt — saying your name. Calling you Kamalakar.'

'It sounds fine — call me Kamal.'

'Oh no. This can't go on. We mustn't let it continue.'

'You're sore with me?'

'Oh no, no, no. Certainly not. It's just what happened.'

'You wanted it to happen — just as much as I wanted it to, didn't you?'

'Yes, I guess so. I've thought about it a lot. I guess we both wanted it. Oh, but it should not happen any more. Not if I'm to stay here.'

'Well, if that's what you want. All right.'

'Oh Kamal, don't be annoyed with me. You know it's not like that at all. It's just that I'm frightened of what will come out of it.'

'Leave that to me.' I took her in my arms.

I got rid of Mrs Khanna and her crowd in less than an hour that night.

Pushpa said, 'Good night, Kamal.'

'How do you get home?' I'd never asked that before, never even wondered.

'I'll take a bus. I live out in Indira Nagar. It takes about half an hour to get there.'

'Why not let me drive you home?'

'It's out of the way for you. I couldn't let you.'

'You must leave that to me.'

She gathered her shawl and her handbag. We walked down together and I helped her into my car. We had supper at the Jewel Box, and it was a little before eleven when we finished. I didn't even know how the time passed. I got to talking about Seema. I didn't try to pretend I was a misunderstood husband or anything like that. I told Pushpa the truth. It was just that Seema and I were not meant for each other.

'Couldn't you get a divorce?'

'I've asked her. Don't worry, I've asked her. It seemed obvious even to Seema that she hasn't been thrilled by me.'

'What does she want if she doesn't want you?'

'I don't know — perhaps her home, her bridge, her knitting work. Me, when she wants me.'

'That sounds terrible.'

'Oh no, it's fine. It's like dashing your head against a stone wall.'

'Couldn't you just get away?'

I wondered that query, and after a moment's pause, said, 'That would be nice, wouldn't it? Seema has her own money. It isn't as if she depended on me. As a matter of fact, I've been dependent on her. It's not as though we have any children — anything to keep us together.'

'Don't you owe yourself anything?'

'I don't know what. Like every lawyer, I've got ambitions. I hope to get to the Supreme Court, some day, or to become a judge at least. Hell, I don't know. But I'm a lawyer. Sometimes I think I'm a lawyer because I need to be. I've been one for fifteen years now. That's as far as I've got. I could throw it all away, and what would I have? I wouldn't even have anything to live on.'

'Don't you have a bank account? Don't think I'm trying to pry.'

'Sure. We've a joint account. Seema might let me go away with another woman, but not with her money. She'd hound me off the edge of the earth.'

'Poor Kamal.'

'Don't feel sorry for me. I've what I asked for.'

'Oh, you haven't. You couldn't possibly have known.'

'No. But now I know.'

'You could be happy. You could be so happy.' Our hands tightened under the table.

'Yes,' I said. 'I could be happy. But only you can make me happy.' I nodded. That was when I knew for certain. She was right. I had to do something.

Back in the car, we sat with only our hands clasped. It was enough for the moment, all the excitement in us met and fused in our fingers. It was odd, the terrible need we felt for each other.

The car raced through the darkness. The sound it made was the only sound on the road. The hum of the motor, and the faint dash of light across us. Nothing else was real. It was as if we were hurtling through space.in a vacuum and nothing extraneous could ever touch us.

FOX THE NEXT FEW DAYS, Pushpa did not mention her troubled friend, and I forgot all about her. I merely kept shuttling between my home and my office. I knew what weighed on my mind, but I kept pushing it out without allowing myself to come to a decision. When I was with Pushpa, I was happy. When I was not, I was obsessed. All I could do was, wonder where she was and what she was doing. I would get to my office early and wait for her.

I had a very nice office. Like everything else Seema had bought for me, it had cost a lot of money — the leather chairs with the correct contours, the low desk and the judge's chair behind it. Everything had a posh, expensive look. I had spent Seema's money extravagantly for the neutral-grey rug, with the pad beneath it. It gave a comfortable feeling under a client's feet. It gave him a feeling of confidence in me. And there was more. They quit thinking in terms of peanuts in fees by the time they'd traversed the distance from the door to chair.

My law library was the best in Bangalore. The Bangalore Bar Association had assessed all its members' requirements a few years ago and built a central law library. It was no better than mine — and its shelves were not half so good.

Oh yes, I was proud of what I possessed and I wanted to keep it. I wanted to improve it. Most days I could shut off my mind. I could consciously block the tensions without taking tranquillizers, which Seema could not do without. I could force myself to forget the things that drove me — the basic needs and hungers that come to a man. Sure, I was being robbed. But every man compromised, did not he? Nobody got everything he wanted. I had Seema and her money. I had my law practice, my library, my reputation in the bar fraternity — among lawyers I was respected and feared. Nobody used gimmicks or tried to pull carpets out from under Kamalakar Sharma.

I stood looking down at the main road. Two million people in a city planned for 60,000. I had what I wanted here in Bangalore, did not I?

And then I could smell Pushpa even before I could hear her on the expensive carpeting.

'I missed you,' Pushpa said.

'I've been waiting for you.'

'I don't live when I'm away from you. I have no life away from this office.'

I drew her close against me, and said, 'We can't go on like this, Pushpa.'

'No,' she agreed.

'I can't endure it.'

'Kamal,' she sighed, 'what are we going to do?'

'I know what I want. I want you. I'd like to go on a honeymoon with you — a long, long one. Maybe for a year. In Japan.'

'Only a year! That's not much of a honeymoon,' she said.

'A year in Japan only,' I amplified.

She laughed. 'Oh, Kamal, what am I going to do? I simply can't live without you. Life is hell for me when I'm away from you.' She rested her head on my chest and put her arms round me. I planted a light kiss on her forehead.

'I think I'll leave Bangalore for a while. Go somewhere far, far away.'

'Do you want me to lose my mind?' I asked in anguish.

'What else is there, Kamal?'

'Don't give up. She can't live for ever.'

'Isn't it terrible, Kamal? But that's what I think. I lie awake at night, turning it over in my mind, again and again. She seems to be immortal.'

'I too seem to feel that.'

'Too bad she isn't dead.'

'Yes.'

'Do you hate me for saying that, Kamal?

'Why should I hate you? It's what I think. It's what we both think.'

It was between us all the time. When we looked at each other, we saw it in each other's eyes. When we spoke, it was behind the most common-place things we said.

'You've got to stop me thinking like this, Kamal.'

'No. It's better now that we've brought it out in the open. What's she got to live for? A bank full of money that she chews like a cow on its cud.'

A tremor went through her and she gripped my arms,

staring into my eyes. 'But — we'll never do it, will we, Kamal?'

'I don't know.'

'Killing somebody... How terrible that is... you don't know.'

I walked away from her and stood at the window. People crawling around down there, walking over each other, snarling. Why did not they kill? Was it because they were afraid?

'You are wrong,' I said. 'I know how terrible it is to kill. But I know something else — how impossible it's getting away with it.'

'We're not going to do it, Kamal. It's insane even to think about it.'

I turned round. 'You're wrong. We are going to do it.'

'We?' she leaned against the desk.

'We. Us. You and I. All we can do now is to figure out how we can do it and get away with it.'

'We couldn't, Kamal,' she shivered. But the look in her eyes was anxiety and compulsion all fused.

'Yes, we have to.'

'How? How could we ever take her life? What's she ever done to us?'

'She's keeping us apart. She's got the money we need.'

'But does she really have to be killed?'

'She's an obstacle. And she's keeping us apart. The way she's living now she's better dead than alive. Don't you think we'd actually be doing her a favour by killing her?'

'Yes, if you say so, Kamal.'

'Sure. She's no good even to herself. We want her money... and we want to get away with it.'

She stood silently against the desk for a long time. At

last she whispered, 'Are you planning an accident, Kamal... perhaps an accidental death?'

I laughed. A sharp, harsh sound I did not recognize. 'You mean, because I am a lawyer? I could beat the accidental death rap? Oh, no. That's too risky. Thank God, I'm a lawyer. I know all the ins and outs, I can tell you. Accidents are never just accidents. Somebody's to blame for every accident — and when there's money involved, somebody will keep picking at the accident. No. The last thing we want is to get 'mixed up with an insurance company or a jury.'

'But you do believe you can help the Khanna woman and her kid?'

'That's different. The risk is theirs. I'm her agent, her representative, and her counsel. Anything I do for her is privileged. Another gimmick lawyers have contrived in courts to be sure justice is the only accident.' I turned round. 'But when I'm personally involved in an accident or a trial, everything changes. Accidents or anything that might involve insurance is out... We've got to have a foolproof design for murder.'

'Is she heavily insured?'

'No, not for a woman with fifty lakhs. There's a great deal more insurance on me.' Again that burst of strange laughter crossed my mouth. 'As a matter of fact, you might profit more by killing me.'

At first her face went white, as if I had struck her. Then she said, her smile uncertain, 'I will, darling, I will. But not with one stroke. Slowly. I'll kill you with my love. I'm going to love you to death.'

'I can't wait to start dying.'

NEXT MORNING, I was waiting for her, when she entered the outer office. I called out to her. She still had her shawl on when she came through the door. I said, 'You want to go through with it?'

She paused, frowning. She bit at her under lip. 'I don't know anything. All I want is you, Kamal. And you know that.'

'Then you want to go through with it?'

She took a deep breath. 'I want to go through with it, Kamal. With you.'

When she stood beside me, her shoulder against my arm, I began talking, fast. Because I wanted to get it all out. Make her understand how clever we were going to be.

'Murder's something that's got to be carefully planned. The design's got to be absolutely foolproof. You can't say that some people get away with murder and take a chance on the law of averages. Averages have nothing to do with it. You can't afford a loss when you mess with murder. And you can't afford a bad guess. You know who gets away with murder? — Professional killers.'

'Really?'

'Because they leave both ends of an alley open. But we are not professionals. Neither can we hire them. It's something we've got to do ourselves. And murder's the biggest crime. We can't just hope to commit a murder and get away with it. Murder's too big, too glaring, has too many people picking at it. We've got to be smart. We can't take the chance of getting involved in a trial. None of those clever angles that might get you free. I've been practising for the past fifteen years in courts. I know what juries are. Juries are prejudices, ignorances, what a man ate for lunch, how he gets along with his wife, what he's got on his mind, and all that rubbish. A jury'll take a liking to the lawyer or an accused, and nothing else is important. I'm not risking my neck to the judgement of twelve stupid people two lawyers have allowed to sit in a jury box. We've got to stay out of court. We've got to fix it so we not only are never caught, but are never even suspected.'

'It won't be easy. It'll take time. And it can't be hurried. If we do it at all, we've got to go slowly, prepare a very fine blueprint for the murder.'

'Oh, Kamal. If we could only run — run away.'

'Sure. Act big, take a big chance. You win big — but you lose big. That's just fine. But I want to keep what I have. I want to stay here, Pushpa. First of all, I want you. I want that money too — and all it'll buy... all I've missed in life. I want to get away with it. I don't even want to be suspected.'

'But is there a way?'

'Sure. I told you. A little at a time. And the good thing about it is you don't have to keep looking over your shoulder.'

'I don't understand.'

'Do you have to?'

'All right, I trust you.' She looked at me straight in the eyes with her eyes sparkling.

I left the office for lunch. I had to get out of there, away from Pushpa, where I could think clearly. Near her, her perfume had a heady effect and made me want to touch her. I walked down the corridor. A man spoke to me twice before I even realized there was anybody else going towards the lift. 'Oh, hello Doctor!'

He laughed, 'Good God, you must've been terribly self-absorded. I've been speaking to you.'

Dr Jagannath had his consulting room on the same floor as my office. He was carrying his medical kit. It appeared he was going on a call. 'You had an appointment with me Kamal over a week ago. I told you, you need a check-up. You've been driving yourself like mad. You can't do that, you know. You're begining to show signs of a breakdown.'

I laughed at him. 'Look who's talking,' I said. 'You need some check-up yourself.'

'With me it's different. I'm run down like this because I don't know any good doctors. You've no excuse — Kamal. You know me. Why don't you drop in tomorrow?'

'Sure.' But I was not going to waste my time in any doctor's clinic. Seema had started this foolishness weeks ago. She had said I was not eating well, that I snapped at her, that I never smiled any more. She had called Jagannath. And he had agreed with her. But I knew that I did not need a doctor, and I knew exactly what I needed.

THAT AFTERNOON I did not return to my office. At six o'clock I walked into the house. It was obvious that Seema was startled to see me. 'Are you well, Kamal?' She put aside her knitting needles and swarmed all over me. I thrust down her soft hands.

'I'm all right.'

'Dr Jagannath called. I believe you've an appointment with him tomorrow.'

'It's not definite.'

'But you've promised to see him. He told me.'

'All right I promised. But I don't want to see him. I don't need a doctor. I know what's wrong with me.'

'What's it, Kamal? Me?' she inquired self-consciously.

I poured myself a can of beer. A tall, cool, beer and drank it off. 'I might as well be honest about it. It's you.

Partly. But of course it's not your fault. You are what you are and I am what I am.'

'What do you want me to be, Kamal? I try. Honestly, I try.'

'Maybe I don't want you to try. Maybe that's it. It's too late to try. I can't help it. I feel absolutely bored when I walk into this place. You bore me to death. You suffocate me. I can't help it, Seema.' I poured myself another beer.

'Please Kamal, you drink too much.'

'Would you believe Seema, I never drink when I'm away from you. I only need a drink when I'm with you.'

She sank down on the sofa. And she ran her fingers nervously over her knitting work. 'Oh, Kamal. Must you hurt me? Do you get any pleasure hurting me? Is that it, Kamal?'

I crossed the room and looked down at her. 'Seema, I don't want to hurt you at all.'

'But you do.'

'Yes, I do. But it's not easy for me, Seema. If only you'd give me a divorce, you'd be out of it.'

'No, Kamal, you'd be out of it. That's what you want.'

'All right. We would both be out of it.'

'But that's just it, Kamal. I don't want to be out of it. If only you'd put off the idea of divorce and all that, we could go away somewhere. Start all over again.'

'I don't want to go away somewhere.'

'You'll get over this, Kamal. You're merely in one of your moods. You've gone through this before and you've got over it.'

I stared at her. *'That just goes to show, Seema,'* I thought, *'you don't know me as well as you think you do.'*

'It's not one of my moods, Seema. I actually mean it.'

I don't want to discuss it.'

'We've got to.'

'Why?'

'Because, otherwise something terrible is going to happen.'

'How can you say that, Kamal? I'm very happy with my life. We've a lovely home. We've nice friends. People speak well of us. I'm very thrilled to be Mrs Kamalakar Sharma.'

I wiped the back of my hand across my mouth.

'Besides, Kamal, I don't believe in divorce.'

'No, you don't,' I barked a laugh at her, full of sarcasm. 'But do you believe in love, Seema?'

She smiled and shook her head.

'I think I suffered from it some years ago. As a matter of fact, we both suffered from it, at the same time, when we were at college. Isn't that so?'

She smiled. 'Now, Kamal. That's better. That's how I like to hear you talk — with a sense of humour.'

'Well what else does one do, bash your head with a hammer?'

You cannot blame me. I'd tried. I did not want to kill Seema, if I could help it. I wanted to be free. Yes, I also wanted her money. But only if I was left with no alternative except to kill her. Had she only been more understanding, I could have settled for my freedom only, and left her alone. This was my last try, and I was not going to give her another chance. What can I do, if she is bent upon digging her own grave!

I did not sleep that night. I planned.

I WAS late at office next morning. Pushpa was waiting for me eagerly. She suggested we have lunch together, but I refused. I told her I had promised to join a client at lunch. 'I don't remember any such appointment,' she said.

I looked up at her. 'There wasn't any. He rang me at home this morning, and I accepted.'

'I'm sorry, Kamal. It's just that ... I don't know why I feel this way. But I feel so frightened sometimes that I may lose you.'

'You must trust me.' I came round the desk and gathered her in my arms. I lifted up her chin and looked deep into her eyes. 'Pushpa, you must try to understand. I'm undergoing a great strain. Good God, do you know what I'm doing? I'm planning a murder… a murder. And it has to be planned so cleverly ... that I've got to use every bit of my wits and commonsense… One false move, and we've both had it. You and I.'

'Oh, I'm sorry Kamal. I was being childish… God knows how much I suffer, when I'm away from you.'

'Only for awhile, darling. After that, just imagine, the whole world would be at our feet. We'll go away from here. At least for some time. We'll go on a cruise — to the South Pacific Islands perhaps… And when we return we'd be new people… all this stinking affair completely forgotten.'

I pressed my body against hers. I felt all the excitement and warmth that charged from her into me. She suddenly became serious, and withdrew herself from me. 'But Kamal, if you do feel I'm making you do terrible things, all for my sake, you can back out, you know… I'll never hold anything against you… I'll go away from here…'

'No, no. Pushpa. You mustn't talk like that. You know that I can't live without you.'

She came into my arms again. Her eyes closed slowly. I planted a long kiss on her soft lips.

THE DINING ROOM was very crowded in the Jewel Box. I spotted Sarita Shah. She was at a corner table all by herself. I knew she usually lunched there.

'Sarita. Sarita Shah!' I took her by surprise. She looked up and stared at me for a moment. Then she stood up and threw up both her hands in excitement.

'Why, Kamal. Kamalakar Sharma,' she gushed.

'Yes, I'm so happy to see you.'

'Oh, you liar. How I love the way you lie. You haven't thought about me in years.'

'Don't be silly.'

'Why don't you join me?'

I picked up the menu, scanned it and ordered something light for myself. As soon as I put the menu down, Sarita took my hand and squeezed it. 'You don't know really how thrilled I'm lunching with you, Kamal.'

I looked at Sarita. And I wondered what she'd have been like, without the beauty salon, the fashion shop and the shoe stables. But it did not matter. She was the supremely smooth result. They bent each brown hair into shape, shaded her eyes and touched up the corners, suggesting depth to their dark brown. They highlighted the planes of her cheeks, and lined her lips. They supported and accented all her natural endowments.

It was not that Sarita Shah was in any sense false. She was well done. The quality that made her different was her inner glow. She gave the feeling that she would smear the lipstick, muss the hair, rip off that dress if the stimulation was there. And better than that, her eyes told you that you — only you — could ever accomplish just that correct stimulation.

My lunch arrived. The waiter started serving me.

I had helped her to get a divorce from Jayant Shah. It could have been messy, but I handled the angles for her. And she never could forget it. It was as if I had saved her life. That was the way she regarded it. And she felt I was somehow responsible for her second chance of happiness.

'What do you do with yourself, Kamal?'

'Oh, I watch Seema do her knitting. I get women out of marriages they thought heaven had got them into.'

'Don't you ever feel lonely?'

'Why should I? Haven't I got Seema?'

'Oh, don't give me that nonsense, Kamal. Not to me, Sarita Shah. I know Seema. I know her well. She's a dear friend. Nevertheless. But for you? Oh, poor Kamal.'

'Let's talk about something else.'

'All right. Read any good books lately?'

'You know, it's nice being here like this with you, Sarita.'

She frowned. A tiny line deepening between her perfectly arched brows. 'Kamal, what lies. Be frank, now. Why are you suddenly so attentive?'

'Not suddenly. I've always loved you, Sarita.'

'Don't hurl that word love around like a low score at golf, Kamal. After I got my divorce from Jay — after you got it for me — I was in a state of, well, upheaval. I needed someone. Someone to make me feel needed. I would've worshipped you — if only you'd been good to me.'

'Oh, Sarita. I couldn't take advantage of you. I thought it'd be in bad taste.'

'In what way? I wanted you, I craved for you. But you'd not a moment for me. Now, all of a sudden, you like being here with me.'

'I'd like being anywhere with you, Sarita.'

Her eyes narrowed slightly. After a few moments, she

said, very softly, 'Would you, Kamal? Would you? Well, we'll just see about that.'

People turned to look at us as we left. I was aware of the whispers. I knew Sarita was. This was what I wanted, and it was almost as though Sarita also suspected it. But that was not what bothered me at all. When I walked back into my office at three, Pushpa was sitting in my judge's chair, awaiting me. She watched me cross the office.

Her voice was cold, and there was disgust in her eyes. 'Who was she?'

'Who?' I tried to smile.

'The woman you lunched with.'

'You sound like a wife.'

'Do I? Well, maybe I do. But there's this to remember, Kamal, and you better remember it. I'm in something with you. It's not exactly a game. I'd like to be able to trust you. How can I, when I see you running around?' Her fangs were showing. She was a different Pushpa now. She was not holding the checkrein on anything at the moment. Her dark eyes blazed. There was hatred in those eyes. I feared she would spring across the desk and claw me.

I laughed. In fact, I felt good. I felt flattered.

'Stop laughing, will you!' She screamed. 'Chasing some woman, behind my back. Thank God, I found out before —'

She jumped up. I took her in my arms. She beat at me and writhed herself free. She tried to run and I caught her, pulling her back. We lost our balance and fell hard on to the leather sofa. She tried to kick and scratch. But I pressed her down. I held her so tightly she could hardly breathe.

She kept twisting her head back and forth, her hair falling free, till I mashed my mouth hard over hers. I held her like that till she stopped struggling. Till her arms tightened around me, and I felt her body quiver.

'Oh, Kamal, you drive me crazy. I go wild. And then you kiss me and I can't fight you any more.'

'You don't have to fight me.'

'Who's she Kamal? She phoned twice — before you returned.'

'I hope you told her I'll return her call.'

'She didn't give me her name. She kept asking if you were back yet.'

'I'm sorry, darling. I should've confided in you. Listen carefully now. I went to Jewel Box purposely today.'

'Who's she?'

'That was Sarita Shah, Pushpa. She'll phone here often. I want you to play it, straight. You're just my secretary as far as Sarita Shah is concerned. And that's all.'

She tried to writhe herself free again. I shoved her back on the couch hard. 'You've got to trust me, Pushpa. You've got to trust me. Remember, we're in it together. The thing I'm planning — it's going to work only if I'm careful. The planning has to be very careful. And Sarita Shah's a part of the planning.'

'I don't know what you're talking about.'

'Then shut up and listen. My plan needs her. I warn you right now, Pushpa, we — I mean you and I — can never be gossiped about — not even once. If even one person suspects we're in love, that's one person too many, and all my planning is destroyed.'

'So you're not involved with her, in any way?'

'Of course not. We've got to be careful Pushpa. You know that. Maybe I've got more to win than you. But Seema has a lot of money, and it goes with me. And once it's mine we're going to enjoy it together.'

'What's this woman Sarita Shah got to do with it?' She tried to thrust upward and free herself.

'Darling, that's it. She's got everything to do with it. You'll see. I don't want to confuse you. But, Pushpa, you've got to trust me. I repeat again and again, I'll never let you down.'

She lay still for a moment, her eyes very pensive. 'Still you must give me some clue as to how she comes into the picture.'

'All right, if you insist. See, I want Sarita Shah to be the reason Seema sues me for divorce.'

'Is Seema planning to divorce you?'

'No. But it's got to look as though she was, if we're to stay on top. And that's why you've got to trust me, and that's where Sarita Shah comes in. Don't you understand?'

'Well, I'm trying to.'

I pressed my mouth over hers, hard. 'You'd better. Starting right now. You'd better.'

She writhed beneath me, but she wasn't trying to free herself any more. The telephone rang stridently.

'There she is,' Pushpa said against my mouth. 'There she is again.'

'Thank God,' I told her. 'Things are working out right — exactly the way I planned.'

WHEN THE EXCITEMENT was enough to make me burst, she sat up and ran her hands through her hair. I could see the smouldering in her eyes. Her dark eyeballs shone like two jewels. They seemed to be swimming and dry at the same time.

She pushed me away.

I stood up and loosened my collar. 'I'm going crazy wanting you. Being put off every time.'

She, too stood up, her voice husky with emotion, 'If you want to know the truth, Kamal, I don't trust you.'

'That's wonderful. And why don't you trust me? Because of Sarita? I told you Sarita means nothing to me.'

'It's not Sarita Shah. It's no one in particular. Not any one thing, but a number of things combined. We're... in something together, Kamal. And we both know, it's for the money and for your freedom — and for each other. But I stand to lose —'

'What are you talking about?'

'I never had anybody in my life. I'm going to have you... But I want to be sure you want me — when it's over.' She grabbed my arms, and those dark eyes gleamed again. 'Do you hear me, Kamal? No matter how long we have to wait... you're going to want me.'

'We can't stampede into this, Pushpa.'

'All right.'

'My God, what do you want? Shall I get a gun and shoot her down? There's the noise, the bullet, the gun itself. Plenty for them to pick at and work on. I don't think we'd get away with that at all.'

'Oh, Kamal. I don't mean anything like that.' Her face was like a white sheet. 'You know what I want, Kamal. I want to belong to you.'

I spoke softly, but in the stillness of the office, I sounded as though I were shouting. 'You can't hurry the process,' I said.

I told her the things I had considered, discarded. A gun was out of the question, because it would turn up. It could be traced. And a knife. I shuddered when I thought about a knife. I could never use one. Even though there was a great deal in favour of a knife. Professional killers used one. They figured in crimes of passion. You could use an ordinary kitchen knife. The kind sold in a thousand stores. And it could never be traced to you. But even talking about it in that office, I seemed to see the gush of blood, smell the sick sweet warmth of it. I could feel the slime that would not wash off.

'Just one spot of blood on you or your clothing,' I said with a shudder, 'and that would be enough for a crime lab.'

'All right, Kamal, I leave everything to you. You decide upon the exact course.'

'There's only one way it can be done — and done so I'm never even suspected.'

I PAUSED outside the smart entrance of Kalpataru department store. I stood on the walk a moment, just thinking about it. Here I was taking the second step towards killing my wife. I was killing Seema right now, right this instant, as surely as if I were choking the breath from her lungs. I had been killing her as I sat in the Jewel Box laughing and chatting with Sarita Shah where Seema's catty friends could see us together.

People stepped around me. They passed on either side of me, hurrying, laughing and chatting. The sun was reflected in the big window. And I stared for a moment at the blaze of the reflected light.

I walked into the store. Women were herding through the aisles. They all looked like Seema. Fat and extravagant. Because they did not have anything else to occupy their minds. I moved slowly towards the sari counter. I wanted to buy Seema a cheap sari. A woman who had been arranging some small packages on the shelves behind the counter was turning towards me, when I changed my mind.

It was a clever thing to buy a sari that was so cheap and so widely sold that it could not be traced anywhere. But was it smart for me to buy it? That foolish woman at the counter might remember I had bought a sari. Even in this enlightened age there was something comic about a man who was doing his wife's shopping.

There was nothing comic about it. But I saw suddenly that I had almost committed my first serious error. I was not allowed any errors in this game. It was all right to buy a cheap sari, but it was not all right for me to buy it. I shook my head and turned to walk away.

'Kamal, Kamalakar!'

I almost walked into Sarita Shah. Silently I thanked God. I had not bought the sari. 'What're you doing in this part of the store, Kamal?' Sarita exclaimed. 'You've got a girl friend, Kamal?'

'Why, no Sarita. Don't you know?'

'I wish I knew Kamal. I've been trying to get you on the phone. I got to thinking after I left you. What you need is to get away from everything — you're too tense. You're worried about something?'

'Me? No. I've no worries.'

'But you look as if you do. What you need is a quiet evening, Kamal. The kind I could arrange for you. A cool drink, no friends, no people at all. Long-playing records, and the lights down, low. How does that sound, Kamal?'

'That sounds fine. When do we meet?'

'Tonight, Kamal? Could you make it tonight?'

'Sounds fascinating. I can't wait.'

'About sevenish.'

I STOOD at the window of my office and stared down at the main street. I did not move till the door opened and Pushpa hurried in. 'Kamal, here it is.'

I turned and she tossed the package from Kalpataru on the desk.

I opened the package, wadded the Kalpataru paper and tossed it into the waste-paper basket.

'What do you plan to do with it, Kamal?'

I did not reply. I opened the box.

'Is it cheap?'

She laughed. 'They manufacture them by the million.'

I opened my filing cabinet and dropped the sari inside. I stood there looking at it. Good-bye Seema. This is really good-bye. I did give you every chance.

'ARE YOU COMFORTABLE, KAMAL?'

Sarita's voice melted and ran down over me like honey. I lay back on her divan. Bathed in the softness of distant indirect lighting, and the soothing whisper of long-playing records, the atmosphere was most romantic. It was all contrived so that I could relax. But I did not. I was sweating with impatience.

'I'm fine, Sarita.'

'You could've been doing this all this time, Kamal. This — and anything else you wanted.' She smoothed her hand along the side of my neck. Her touch was soft. Her fingers barely caressed me. And at first it had been faintly pleasant. Now I felt as though months were wearing me raw.

'That's the way it is. A man can't help being blind.'

'Are you deaf too, Kamal?'

'No. Just dumb.' I closed my fingers on her hand stilling it for a moment. 'Why Sarita?'

'Do you think I want anyone but you, Kamal? You think I ever have?'

'I don't know.'

'Then you're a fool. I couldn't want anyone else the way I want you. That's why I'm so anxious to tell you... I'm going out of town for a week, Kamal.'

'Do you consider it good news?'

'It is, unless you deliberately fail to understand. Kamal.'

Her fingers moved along my neck again. 'I'm leaving in the morning — for Madras. Maybe you can also plan a business trip outside Bangalore — perhaps to Madras — day after tomorrow, Kamal.'

'That sounds fine, Sarita. I don't know. But it's awfully sudden.'

'Oh stop, Kamal. You take business trips all the time. I know. You could get away if you wanted to.'

'Of course, I want to. But I'll have to check.'

'You won't have any regrets, Kamal. I promise you. I'll make you very, very happy.'

'I already know that.'

'Promise.'

I stalled her. I did not want to make her too certain I would go. That would make her too careful about her arrangements — too secretive. That was the last thing I wanted — besides Sarita Shah.

I stopped at the first public phone booth on my way home. I got inside, closed the door, and dialled. The phone rang many times. No response. I sweated. Where was Pushpa? Why was not she home?

'Hello,' Pushpa's voice had sleep and warmth in it. The

kind of warmth that surged through those wires and got inside me.

'Listen to me. You come up with a story about a sick aunt somewhere. Spread the word around to anybody who might be interested. Pack up. I want you to get ready to fly to Delhi.'

'Why?'

'Because Sarita Shah's going to Madras.'

'What has that got to do with us?'

'Everything. Whenever she leaves town, you and I can leave town. Pack up. I'll see you at the office in the morning. And I'll explain everything.'

WHEN SARITA SAW me at the Railway Station the following morning at nine, something happened to her face. She blushed. She looked as confused as a teenager She stared first at my face, then at the travelling bag I carried.

'Kamal, are you taking this train?'

'Aren't you?'

'Yes, I told you I was. But is this — very discreet?'

I grinned, 'Maybe not. But what difference does it make?'

For a moment she frowned. She looked about the platform. A bevy of her friends were pouring through the gate to bid her good-bye. 'You've got to be careful, Kamal. Please. I'll see you on the train.'

Careful was the last thing I wanted to be at the moment. But I did not say anything about that to Sarita. She had an odd look on her face. Almost as if she had over-estimated me. It appeared as if she suddenly doubted many things she had believed about me.

Only one thing annoyed me. There were not many of Seema's friends at the station.

I travelled with Sarita to Madras, and on reaching there I took the first available flight to Delhi.

Pushpa was waiting in her room at the Ashoka Hotel. I registered. I was impatient with the time it took me to sign my name and go through the motions of looking at the room assigned to me.

I knocked on the door. She threw it open instantly. She was wearing no make-up. Her hair was down, around her shoulders. She was wearing a bright negligee that caught about her waist. 'Oh, Kamal. I didn't expect you so soon?'

'Do you throw your door open to every man who knocks like this?'

She laughed and drew me inside. 'How was the trip?'

I was looking at her, at her things, scattered intimately about the room, the perfume of her lotions on the dresser.

'Boring,' I said. 'Sarita was afraid people were going to talk about us. I think she's very disappointed in me. Even when I told her I was changing trains in Madras, had a couple of day's work in Bombay, she still felt that people at home wouldn't know that — and were going to talk.'

Without moving consciously, we drew close together. I pressed my hands tightly on Pushpa's negligee.

'I wish we could stay like this all the time. You do love me?'

'What did you tell Seema?'

'What do I ever tell Seema? That I had business out of town. She'll have to accept it.'

'What are people going to think? You and I both gone from the office?

'What can they think? After the way I scurried into the train with Sarita, they won't have time to talk about you.'

'I love you, Kamal. I'm crazy about you. Kamal, I love you. Kamal.'

I walked all round Connaught Circus and its department stores. I kept telling myself that New Delhi was unbelievably vast, the odds against seeing anyone I ever knew were staggering. Yet it seemed to me that Pushpa was taking hours over some simple purchases.

We had walked through the road and I had told her in detail the things I wanted. 'Keep them simple. And don't buy the handbag or the shoes unless there are at least six others like them on the racks. Get the cheapest under-clothing.'

I watched the cars and the people pass me. I sweated. I had used a phoney name in the hotel register. I could swear I had not been in Delhi. Nobody could prove otherwise. Nevertheless I was worried. You had to think of everything, when you wanted to commit a murder.

'Kamal.'

I heeled round. Pushpa was standing there loaded with packages. She looked young and fresh. She looked almost like a young housewife out shopping for bargains.

'You took long enough.'

'Kamal, you can't buy even cheap things in a hurry. You have to select carefully.'

We stared at each other. For an instant all the sounds of the busy street faded and we were alone in the stillness. She shook her head. She said, 'I hope the under-things fit Seema. I didn't know her exact size. I made a rough guess.'

The sense of chill deepened. I looked around and waved at a taxi. My voice sounded odd. 'Seema won't care.'

I got back to Bangalore late on Monday night. I hoped I could get quietly into the house and into my bedroom. I did not see how I could face a session with Seema till I had had a few hours sleep alone.

The lights were on in the front room. Seema was lying on the divan, sipping a glass of Coca-Cola. She stared up at me. 'Did you have a good time?'

'Was I supposed to?'

'How was she?'

'Who?'

'Stop trying to play innocent with me.'

'I'm not. It's too late to play anything.'

'Sure. Too late. And too tired. I hate it when you try to play innocent with me.'

'Look, I'm not playing innocent. I'm tired. I want to go to bed.'

'Go to bed.' She sat up and threw the glass at me. It struck the door at the side of my head. She spat: 'Sarita Shah!'

'What are you talking about?'

'You know what I'm talking about. I'm talking about Sarita Shah in the city of Madras.'

'So?'

'So I don't believe you went to Delhi on business.'

'Oh, you're a real fool.'

'Am I? And you're not?'

'I'm not trying to be.'

'With Sarita Shah, in Madras. Tell me. What's she like when she bursts out of her brassiere?'

'I don't know what you're talking about.'

She looked round for something else to throw.

'Oh, I know about you and Sarita. Barrister Kamalakar Sharma, the big name in Bangalore, in a cheap hotel room in Madras, with that whore Sarita Shah...'

'Listen Seema, if I wanted to have an affair with Sarita,

why should I go with her to Madras. I could have had it right here, in Bangalore.'

'You wouldn't dare. You wouldn't dare to take the risk…'

'All right, if you think I'm having an affair with that Shah woman… maybe you're right. But then Seema why don't you sue me for divorce?'

She began to laugh, hysterically. That laugh made me shiver. She lay back, wagging a finger. 'That's why I stayed awake to see you, Kamal. I wanted to tell you. If you're trying to force me to divorce you, by those methods, it won't work. I won't do it. I don't want to tarnish my family name. But then, remember, you have a career. If only for the sake of your precious career, you might have sense enough to be discreet.'

PUSHPA WAS RECLINING on the divan in my office. 'But Bombay,' she said, 'why must I fly to Bombay?'

'I think it's best, Pushpa. We can't go on like this right here. We can't be seen together anywhere. I'm going nuts.'

'You want to get rid of me?'

'No, certainly not. I want you for always. But I told you it couldn't be a quick thing. It's all a part of my plan. You must help me. And you mustn't ask too many questions. It'll only confuse you.'

'But Kamal, I'll be hundreds of miles from you. I don't know what'll happen here.'

'Don't you trust me?'

'I do. I do. But I keep remembering Sarita Shah. Seema might not mind your being seen around with Sarita Shah, but I do… though I know it's all a part of your plans. I don't think I can stand it. And now you want me to go away for two months to Bombay. Why can't I go to a place nearby, say Mysore?'

'Sure. But it'll be out of character. Too risky, and not the sort of place Seema would go to. She's supposed to be heartbroken when she finally leaves me.'

'And I've got to stay up there for two whole months.'

'Certainly not. We'll try to cut it shorter. Depending on how cleverly you handle your part.'

'What do I do exactly?'

'You register at the Taj Mahal Hotel as Mrs Kamalakar Sharma...'

'That part I like best.'

'Then, after two or three days you get a lawyer. I could send you to one, but it's best you get one yourself. Talk around in the bars, talk to other women, be seen around places where it counts, picture galleries, public functions, cocktail parties. Always introduce yourself as Mrs Kamalakar Sharma. Get a lawyer who's interested in the fee, been in the racket a long time so he's not too particular about your bonafides. There are plenty of them there. Let him put up the case. Any grounds will do, but nothing spectacular. When everything is set and the lawyer tells you he doesn't need you till hearing time, you come back here. Tell him to notify you at the hotel by mail when you're expected to appear. That'll be all right with him.'

'What happens if they found out I was a fraud?'

'They won't.'

'Suppose they do?'

'Leave that to me.'

'Suppose somebody up here finds out?'

'They won't.'

'Suppose the lawyer writes to me about the case at Bangalore as Mrs Kamalakar Sharma.'

'That's where we use our wits. When you see the lawyer the first time, you simply tell him my address is at the moment unknown. That you'll supply it later — and I swear to you, by the time any correspondence starts arriving from him — Seema will be out of the way.

'You swear, Kamal?' She was trembling on my arms.

I held her close. 'It'll all be over, and if we work it right, nobody will suspect anything.'

'But I'll be gone for so long.'

'When it's over, Puspha, we'll be on top of the world, together.'

'But down there, by myself — when will I see you?'

I laughed. 'That's easy. You'll see me as Sarita Shah decides to leave town.'

A week later, I was in Bombay. I hurried from a plane at the Santa Cruz Airport and inquired about the limousine service to the city. When I was told that it was not available, I hired a cab. We raced across the streets into the city, but it seemed to me we were crawling. I could not stay away from Pushpa any more. Her letters, brief and unsatisfactory, left me hungry and despairing.

When I finally reached the city, I got myself a room at the Hotel Nataraj. I registered as Dinanath Kapur, from Rohtak, Haryana. I was only a few furlongs from the Taj Mahal Hotel. But I could not barge in at her place in the middle of the afternoon. She was playing the role of the wife driven to divorce. She would play it very well. I knew. And I was not going to spoil it by playing a reunion scene.

I stalked about inside my air-conditioned room. I turned on the TV. The programme was boring and so I turned it off. The walls closed in on me. Though Puspha was so near, both of us were very alone.

I picked up the receiver and asked the operator to get me the Taj Mahal Hotel. The Taj operator responded. When I gave Pushpa's room number, the telephone rang a few times. Finally, she answered. My heart leapt at the excitement in her tone. 'Kamal. For goodness sake, Kamal. Where are you?'

'A few furlongs from you.'

I walked along Marine Drive, feeling a sense of mounting expectancy. When I reached the end of the road at Nariman Point, I hailed a cab.

IN THE CORRIDOR of the Taj Mahal Hotel, I paused for a moment. I did not want anybody to pass me by, and regard me more as a thief, searching for Pushpa's room number. I wanted to appear cagey, as if I had a room in the corridor. I heaved a sigh of relief, and I had taken a few steps, looking on both sides for Pushpa's room number, when a door opened and light sprayed across me. I stood still.

'Friend, just a second friend.'

A man strolled through the door, leaving it open. I told myself I was scared unnecessarily. But I could not escape the feeling that something had gone wrong.

It would go all wrong. I asked myself coldly what difference it made if this man looked at me, remembered me, a thousand miles from Bangalore. I could not answer that. But I could not prevent the feeling of panic either. He stood looking at me, for a long time. He was dark, tall and well built. His black hair was waved and he had a trim moustache.

I reminded myself I had nothing against his good looks, or the fact that he could afford to stay at a luxury hotel. What I disliked was the knowing leer in his dark eyes and the way his mouth twisted. It was as if he implied I was here stealthily and that I despised being caught like this, pinned in the light from his doorway. I brushed the thought away. What business was it of his if I came to visit a woman across the corridor?

Still, if anything went wrong, he could testify, I had been down here in Bombay to visit Pushpa, only her name was Mrs Kamalakar Sharma. The last thing I wanted was for anyone to think I ever visited Seema down here after she finally left Bangalore for the divorce, that Pushpa and I were getting in her name.

'Got a match?' he asked.

His voice was low and modulated. Ordinarily I would not have given a man like that a second thought. But I did not want him nibbling at me in the next few weeks.

'No,' I said. 'I'm sorry. Oh perhaps you can help me.'

'Sure. You looking for somebody?'

'Yes. A Mr Vikram Cheddah in Room Number 612.'

'If there's anybody by that name in the hotel I wouldn't know. But you're on the wrong floor. 612 should be on the sixth floor. This is the seventh floor.'

'That's it then, I'm on the wrong floor.'

'You sure are. You don't have a match?' I shook my head again, turned and walked back towards the lift. Standing by the lift, I paused and watched him. He went back into his room and closed the door.

Sweating, I returned to the corridor and walked rapidly along it. I found Room 712. It was directly across from his room. I knocked gently. After a moment, Pushpa opened the door. I pushed past her and closed the door behind me.

Before I even spoke to her, I crossed and pulled the venetian blind shut so hard that the slats vibrated.

She was wearing a sheer black negligee I had presented to her in Bangalore. She was standing in the middle of the room, frowning faintly. I went up to her and pulled her to me. For a long time we stood holding each other. She whispered, 'I've been missing you. I've been missing you very much.'

'Who's the gigolo across the corridor?' I asked.

She tilted her head back. 'What an old-fashioned expression!' was all she said.

'He's an old-fashioned type. He looked me over, well.'

'He doesn't matter, darling. He doesn't count. We don't know who he is. You're all tense. You don't even seem glad to see me.'

I caught her so tightly she could scarcely breathe. 'I'm glad, though I don't look it. I can't help the tenseness. It's this business we are both in.'

'Let me look at you Kamal. It's been so long.'

We forgot the man across the corridor, Seema and Sarita Shah, and everything else beyond that locked door. It was worth coming to Bombay just to be with her. That was worth everything.

I left Pushpa at two in the morning. As I walked back to the Nataraj, I paused in the shadows. A blue Fiat, with a Bihar number plate was parked at the kerb. I took out a screwdriver I had bought, went behind the car and knelt against the bumper. It took about two minutes to remove the number-plate. I shoved it along with the screwdriver into a brown paper bag I had brought with me.

I straightened up then and walked quietly through the shadows. All round there was complete darkness and strong silence.

When I reached Bangalore, I stopped off at the office on my way home from the airport. I added the number-plate to the other things I had collected so far. For a long time, I stood looking at the things I had accumulated: the sari, under-clothing, shoes, handbag and now a number-plate from a Bihar car.

Seema came into my bedroom while I was undressing for bed. 'What a delightful surprise,' she said. 'At first I thought it was a burglar.'

'You're not that lucky.'

'Did you hear the news?'

'What news?'

'About Narayan Prasad?'

Narayan Prasad was a friend of mine who had, been appointed the judge of the District and Sessions Court. 'No,' I said. 'I haven't seen a newspaper.'

'Doesn't Sarita give you time to read the papers?'

'What's this about Sarita, now?'

'Nothing. Just that she was out of town this week. Isn't that a delightful coincidence?'

I stepped into my pyjamas. 'What about Narayan?'

'He died of a heart attack.'

I sat down on the bed. Narayan was a year older than I was. When your friends begin dropping dead around you, you begin to worry.

'You should be more careful about the way you carry on with Sarita Shah. You should have more respect for your position. People are talking.'

I told myself, nothing could please me more.

Sabapathy Naidu grinned, got up from behind his desk when I stepped into his office. He was the most prominent dealer in second-hand cars in Bangalore. As always he was chewing *pan* and a red streak of the juice ran down his mouth. He was in his thirties but had a rugged, lined face that appeared much older.

There were three or four salesmen in his office. I had seen a couple more hanging around outside as I came through. Sabapathy was a sharp operator, a dangerous man to do business with unless you understood mechanics and loan-shark financing. Few people understood both and he did a big trade.

I shook hands with Sabapathy, glancing at the salesmen still loitering inside the office. 'All right, all right, you fellows. Get some money coming in. What do I pay you for?'

We all knew Sabapathy Naidu never paid a salary to anybody except the girls in his finance office and the men who washed the cars and swept the premises. But the salesmen grinned and left. They had it good with Sabapathy Naidu. In Bangalore when anybody thought of used cars, they thought of him. That was the way he advertised himself in every newspaper and on the radio.

'Sit down. Sit down. I'll get you a cup of coffee.' Sabapathy squatted in the swivel chair, behind his desk and pressed the call bell. A peon entered, and Sabapathy asked him for two cups of coffee.

'What exactly do you need, Counsellor? Is it a car, or is there anything else I can do for you?'

'I need a little information, Sabapathy.' This was not true. What I wanted was to buy a second-hand car. But I was not going to buy it from Sabapathy Naidu. It had to come from farther away than he got his cars.

'You need it, you name it,' he said. He thrust another *pan* into his mouth, and spoke with his eyes fixed on me. 'How about a little party, Counsellor? You know I've been promising to fix you up with a nice friendly girl. You've done me a big favour. I don't forget things like that. What kind do you like? Thin? Fat? Old? Young? They all come to me sooner or later to buy a car. And I haven't met one yet that didn't want to try it out in the big tracks. Once out there, they want to test the back seat. Once they've been in the back seat with Sabapatby Naidu, they're hooked.

'I tell you, I don't know what's happening to the younger men. I'm worried about the future generation of this country. Young fellows are not like you and me, I tell you. I've got young salesmen working for me, good looking lads in their twenties who ought to be in their prime... But look at them, just look at them.... Oh now, we're side-tracking.

'Counsellor, what has brought you to me, please come straight to the point. I'll do anything for you. You know that. I'm in your debt.'

Sabapathy had got into a serious jam about a year before and had come to me sweating blood. It was the only time I ever knew him to forget to talk about women and his prowess with them. He had bought a couple of stolen cars and the CID got him. He knew he was booked for the jail. He kept yelling that a reputable dealer could not help getting rocked once in a while.

We went to court, and the only thing that saved Sabapathy was that I was able to prove that one of the Government's witnesses was such an unsavoury character that his evidence was no good in any court. Through lack of prosecution evidence, Sabapathy had been released.

'Sabapathy,' I said watching him, 'I don't need anything

or fat woman today — I want the name of the man who runs the hot-car ring you deal with.'

I had socked it to him hard and he sat back looting as though I had struck him. He looked at me distastefully for some time. 'Counsellor, I don't know what to say.'

'His name.'

'Now, look here.'

'No. You look here. This is us, Sabapathy. You and I. You think I thought you were innocent when I got you off? Don't make me laugh. Those CID boys had you by the short hair —'

'And they'd get me again if I fooled around with any hot-car ring.'

'Look Sabapathy, I'm in a hurry. Now deal from top of the deck, or the next time somebody blows the horn on you, you can get yourself another lawyer.'

'Now, Counsellor —'

'That's the way it is. You're always talking about owing me something. Now, I need to know the name of this man.'

'Good Lord, Counsellor, if anything happened to this man, and they ever found out I'd breathed his name — even in my sleep — they'd flay me — just flay me.'

'Nothing is going to happen to him. I need to know the top fellow, because I've got a case that's going to need some tricky work. I may not even get in touch with him. But I want his name.'

Back at my office I put through a trunk call to the name Sabapathy had given me. It was not easy to get through to this fellow, even when I had his personal telephone number. Four men wanted to know where I got that number before I could talk to the big shot.

We spent a long 20 minutes sparring. I told him I

wanted to buy a three-year-old second-hand car either blue or black, and not freshly painted.

Six times, he told me I was crazy, that I had the wrong number. But I was patient. And I mentioned a good price.

'What did you say your name was?'

'Dinanath Kapur,' I told him.

'Yeah. That's good Punjabi name. How I know you're not trying to spring a trap on me.'

'On the telephone? Say you never spoke to me. If you don't have the car I want, forget it. But if you do, deliver it to the Webbs Garage in Bangalore. Leave it in the name of Dinanath Kapur.'

'Suppose I did that? How do I get the money?'

'Cash. The best way there is. By telegraph. Give me any address and I'll send it.'

He thought that over for a long time. Finally, he told me to send the money to Mehmood Hussain, care of the Postmaster of Secunderabad. I wrote that down and that was the first and last time Mehmood and I talked to each other... .

Next morning, I attended the funeral of Narayan Prasad, with Seema. Every important lawyer in the State was there. The Governor spoke a few words. The smell of the flowers was oppressive. I thought about Sarita Shah. The way she spilled out of those foundation garments, the oppressive sweetness, the way she crowded you every moment you were near her. I glanced at Seema. I could not help admitting to myself that she was a lot better than Sarita in every respect.

I was astonished to see Sarita there among the mourners. It had not occurred to me that she might know Narayan Prasad. She was in the Governor's party. And she looked chic and correct.

Seema saw me looking at Sarita and I heard her sigh.

During the lengthy ritual, I could feel Sarita glancing at me. I did not look her way again. I knew that people were whispering. Gossip had built up in the past few weeks. They were pitying Seema. Mentally, I invited anyone of them to step into my shoes and then criticize me. Though it was a joke to think I would ever spend five minutes in Sarita's company when I did not have to. But what these gossips did not know was not going to hurt me.

I was very upset by Narayan Prasad's death. That sounds senseless, being moved by a natural death when I was thinking how soon I was going to kill my wife. But I could not help it. Narayan had been a fine man, with a brilliant career ahead of him.

We drove home in silence.

'Sarita looked very sleek.' Seema said. 'I didn't know she was a friend of the Governor.'

'Neither did I.'

'My! She doesn't tell you much about herself. What's the matter? Don't you talk much?'

I pulled into the driveway, hearing the tyres scrape on the gravel. I stopped the car. Seema began to get out. I put my hand on her arm. 'Seema, I've something to tell you.'

'You don't have to tell me anything. I know everything there's to know. Much more than I want to know.'

'No, this is something else. Something different. This has no business with Sarita. I admit I got mixed up with her. I mean — she threw it at me. It was a mistake. She talks too much. She's too much trouble. The whole thing was wrong.'

'I could've told you that.'

'I had to find out for myself.'

'What I want to know is, what's par for the course,

Kamal? How many of these women do you have to make a fool of yourself over before you grow up?'

I stared out of the window. 'I don't know Seema. That's up to you.'

'Up to me? What are you talking about?'

'I don't know Seema. I'm tired. I'd like to get away. This sudden death of Narayan has upset me.'

'Getting old?'

'Something like that. Anyhow, if you'd go away with me, we could have — a second honeymoon.'

Her smile was sardonic. 'I think you are too worn out for any honeymoons.'

I shrugged. 'We were so happy, once, Seema.'

'Yes, but I can hardly remember that far back.'

'You don't want to try?'

'I try all the time. I'm the only one who tries at all.' She wiped the tears from her eyes. 'Then when you find that another tramp is just a tramp and want to run away — I'm supposed to leap eagerly at the chance.'

'All right,' I said. 'Forget it.'

She sat there a moment. Finally, she sighed. 'Where would you like to go, Kamal?'

'Would you like to fly to Kashmir?'

'You know I don't like to fly,' she said.

'I don't know if you'd like to do it,' as though I had just thought of it. 'But remember our honeymoon?'

She laughed. 'In that old car of yours? We made a tour. We were heading for Kashmir. But it broke down in Nagpur.'

'I couldn't help it. I was broke.' I touched her arm. 'We could do it again, Seema. You and I. Just driving around.'

'Oh, Kamal.' She burst out crying, 'Would you, Kamal? Just you and I? Oh, I'd love that. But let's not drive. We'll do it all by train. Let's do the whole country. Why just Kashmir?'

'Yes, we shall.'

I stared above her head. I knew she would be willing to go, but what I did not know was that she would be so eager to do so. This was just what she wanted. And she could not wait to get started.

SEEMA SPENT the rest of the afternoon and most of the evening talking on the telephone. Too many people had come, in a friendly manner, to cut her pins from under her with stories about Sarita Shah and me. When she phoned, she never mentioned Sarita's name or what they may have said to her. Usually she was just phoning, she said, to cancel an engagement in the immediate future, since she would not be in town. 'Kamal and I are going away on an extended trip. He insisted I go with him. Just wouldn't take no for an answer.'

I sat around with her, letting her stroke my shoulders, or pat my hair as she walked past me, humming a tune. I never wanted a drink so badly in my life. But I did not dare have one. What was ahead was too tricky!

About nine o'clock Seema's closest friend, Manjari Sarkar, came over from next door. She was about four years older than Seema. She and Seema walked all over the house discussing the trip Seema and I were taking. They scoured closets, rummaged walnut chests, drank coffee in the kitchen, while making lists of all that Seema should remember to take with her.

Considering it was about eleven, it seemed Seema and

her friend were going to sit up all night. I was drawn so fine, their voices twanged my nerves like guitar strings.

When she was leaving, Manjari looked up at me, one of those 'Bless you' smiles wreathing her face. 'I'm so glad for you, Kamal. For you and Seema.'

'Sure,' I said. 'Maybe Seema and I haven't got along too well here lately, but with some luck — everything's going to be different.'

Seema's head jerked up. I saw the hurt in her eyes, as if she wished I had not said that. But I had to say it.

By 1.30 A.M. Seema was finally asleep in her room. I listened at her door. Her breathing was deep, as though she were really sleeping soundly for the first time in weeks. Something kept nagging me. Through my mind ran the thought that it was not still too late to call a halt.

I had to remind myself of Pushpa up there at the Taj Hotel in Bombay, and how at last I shall be free to make her mine.

I looked about the house. I was not going to lose any of this. I was going to keep it all. The only difference was that Seema would not be in it — the greatest improvement on the house.

I walked along the foyer, dialled a cab company and spoke as softly as I could, ordering a taxi to pick me up as soon as possible at the Bhashyam Circle.

I left all the lights on, and softly closed the front door behind me.

There was a rising breeze. The whole street was dark. I went swiftly to the corner of the pavement. Somewhere in the darkness a dog barked.

I waited about five minutes and then the taxi swung round the circle and stopped for me. I told the driver my office address downtown and sat back, suddenly chilled in the warm cab.

I went up the lift in the building, in which everything was deathly still. The whine of the cables and the clink of the chains were loud in the shaft.

I let myself into my office and snapped on my desk lamp. For a moment I paused, looking at everything, thinking how much it had cost Seema, how much I had cost her. And I learned right there that it is one thing to think about killing someone, to wish her dead, and it is something else to know the moment has come. You cannot turn back. Not if you want the things you have told yourself you want. But you know from this moment you are no longer Kamalakar Sharma, Barrister-at-Law, you are a killer. A murderer. It does not matter whether or not you get away with it. It does not matter what anyone else in the world thinks about you. It is what you know yourself.

Angrily I pulled open the filing cabinet and gathered up the things I had been accumulating there — the sari, the under-things, the number-plate, the handbag, the shoes and the screwdriver. I put them in a large brown envelope and left.

A young boy was the only attendant on duty at the Webbs Garage. He was sleepy and barely glanced at the flimsy disguise I had worn for his benefit: my reading glasses, my hair brushed back and the pencilline moustache I had painted in a hurry.

I gave him my name as Dinanath Kapur and told him that a car had been left for me. He stared at me for a moment. I felt my pulse quicken. Then he nodded. 'Oh yes, Mr Kapur. It's the black Fiat, right?'

'Right.'

He consulted a chart. 'We serviced it, Sir, filled it with petrol, oil and water.'

'Oh thanks.'

He brought the car and it was exactly what I had hoped for. It was black, apparently in good shape, but a car that you would not remember two minutes after you passed it.

I tipped him, paid him for the servicing and drove out. The car ran smoothly. I drove slowly till I found a dark, uninhabited block on the outskirts of the town, by the side of a stream.

I stopped the car, removed the old number-plate, and threw it into the stream. Then I replaced it with the Bihar number-plate I had stolen in Bombay. If they ever did try to trace this thing — the car, the number plate and title — somebody was going to have a fit.

I drove home, turning off the lights before I reached my driveway. I went as quietly as the car would purr into the darkness beside the car port. Before I went into the house, I got some water from the hose and washed off the service sticker. That was one little item I was not going to forget.

I went into the house carrying the clothes. My arms felt leaden. And my legs seemed to be collapsing under me. I placed the clothing on the floor outside Seema's room. Cautiously I opened the door, stepping to the side to stand in the darkness for a moment. In the stillness, I could hear that dog barking again. 'Seema,' I said, keeping my voice very low.

I could see her now, heaped under the sheets on the bed. She stirred restlessly, and I held my breath, watching.

'Seema, you awake?'

She rolled her head again and I moved forward. Stealthily. I was trembling all over. My hands shook.

I stood beside her bed. And I gently lifted the covers,

putting them over her shoulders and patting them tightly along her body. When she started to writhe, the covers would pin her arms against her, and she would roll herself up in them.

I moved up beyond her head and stood looking down at her for a moment. Good-bye Seema. I had despised her for years, but right then I pitied her, because in a moment she was going to be dead.

I lifted one of her pillows, folded it slightly and pressed it down on her face. I then moved fast. Closing my arms round the pillow, I held it as tightly over her face as I could, pressing it down with all my might.

She hurled herself upward and I let her make a half turn to the right, fighting like a hooked shark. Then I wrenched her back the other way, and her body got tangled in the bed clothes.

She writhed and twisted for a long time. My leaden arms grew weak and I was afraid she would fight herself free. I did not know it would take so long for her to suffocate. It was as if time stopped and she fought to live. Her body rolled back and forth. She tried to fight her arms free. I heard her loud gasps as she tried to breathe through the pillow.

Finally, it ended. Her movements weakened and her hands twitched and then there was no movement at all.

I flopped forward across her. I did not know how long I stayed there. She was completely still. A lifeless mass on the bed.

Suddenly sobs wracked me. I sobbed, not knowing what I was crying for. Maybe for Seema. Maybe for all the miserable unhappy people on earth. But mostly for myself, for Kamalakar Sharma, murderer.

At last I got up and staggered into her bathroom. I was sick.

When I came out, I was feeling faint. I was shaking all over. And just knowing I had to touch Seema's body again, had to dress her in the cheap nameless clothes I had bought for her, made my stomach tighten into knots all over again.

Somehow I did it. Sweat dripped from me, and my fingers shook, reacted clumsily. But I got the underthings and the sari on her. Then I carried her downstairs. She hung limply, her arms dragging on the floor. Twice I almost dropped her.

I laid her out on the back seat of Fiat, I had just got. She looked as though she were fast asleep. Only there was no pulse, no heart beat, no life. I kept telling myself I was free of Seema.

I looked at my watch. It was almost 3.30 A.M. Two hours since Seem a had finally fallen asleep. It seemed as long as half a lifetime.

I felt a quickening of that old panic. Time was something you could not plan in advance, not in a thing like this. I ran back into the house, looked around to be sure I had not left anything. Then I locked the back doors, making certain that Manjari Sarkar would not drop in before I got back.

I was almost at the front door when a bell began ringing shrilly. The sound clattered in my brain. I stared at the front door.

It took me almost a full minute to realise it was the telephone, and not the front door.

I TRIED to make up my mind whether to answer the phone or not. Who could be phoning me at 3.30 A.M. in the morning? Had Manjari Sarkar heard me moving around over here and decided we had burglars? It was better not to answer it at all. Then I thought of Pushpa. Maybe something has gone wrong. I had to answer it.

I raced towards it, afraid now it would stop ringing before I could lift the receiver.

'Hello.' My voice was so hoarse and breathless I hardly recognized it.

'Kamal. Darling. Did I wake you?'

'Who's speaking?'

'Why, Sarita sweetheart. Don't you recognize my voice?'

Impatience flooded through me. That honey-dripping voice of hers made me sweat. I gripped the receiver, waiting to slap it back in its cradle.

'Good lord Sarita, you know what time it is, 3.30 A.M.!'

'Yes I know. I just got home. I thought you'd be glad I phoned you.'

'I am glad. Good-night Sarita!'

Her laugh stopped me. 'You better hear me out.'

'All right, what's it?'

'I must see you at once.'

'It's impossible, Sarita. I'm going out of town right away.'

'You better forget it, and come over here.'

'I can't talk any more.'

'Not even about Narayan Prasad's job?'

It was as if she had clobbered me on the head. I hit against the wall and I was afraid I was going to be sick again.

'I just left Raj Bhavan darling. The Governor gave a

banquet. They were talking about Narayan Prasad's job. And they mentioned you.'

I still could not speak. The words stuck in my throat.

'Did you hear me Kamal? They talked about you for District and Sessions Judge.'

I made a sound in my throat. I do not know what Sarita thought I said. She laughed. I barely heard her. I was standing there in the darkness seeing Seema writhing and fighting me on that bed. Fighting to live. And suddenly it was as if she had been fighting for me instead of against me. She had been fighting to stay alive so that I could have that judgeship — something I wanted with all my heart.

'You're not the only one they mentioned, darling. Don't think it was that simple. But I know the right people, Kamal. The right people and the right things to say. I don't suppose you ever imagined I was capable of doing something like this for you.'

'No.'

'Of course you didn't. You just thought I was good for bed. Isn't that what you thought, Kamal?'

'Yes.'

She laughed. 'I'm good for that too.'

I was thinking about that appointment to Narayan's unexpired term on the bench. One of those foolish, impossible things that could happen. The right politics, being in the right place at the right time.

I thought of the dead body in the car. 'Oh God,' I thought.

'Don't you think you better come here, Kamal? There's so much we've got to talk about.'

'I can't.'

'Kamal, I think you better be nice to me... nicer than you've been. A chance like this won't come again.'

'No.'

'You can have that job, Kamal. The right word from me, and it's yours. But I'm not just making you a present of a peach like that, Kamal.'

'No.'

'No, you're so right. So come on over.'

'What about Seema?'

She laughed. 'What about Seema? I think you're going to divorce Seema, Kamal. I've thought so for a long time. I was suspicious of you from that first day you started paying too much attention to me in public. You were using me. Using me to make Seema lose face, and force her to divorce you. Oh, I knew, Kamal. I wasn't born yesterday. I'm not stupid. I knew you were using me, but I didn't mind. As long as I was getting ... well, part of what I wanted from you. And as long as there was a chance that when you were free... well, we'll talk about that, Kamal.'

Slowly, the blood began to move in my veins again and my pulse quickened slightly. Maybe there was a chance out of this. Maybe I could still have this impossible prize.

If I could make Sarita believe that I was going to divorce Seema, stall her long enough to finish my plan and return to Bangalore, I might still win everything!

'Seema and I — we're getting a divorce, Sarita. But that's for you alone to know. If you repeat...'

'Darling! Why should I? Just now, when there mustn't be a breath of scandal if you're to get that appointment. I'll be discretion itself. That's why I want to see you now. In the dark of night so no one will suspect. I can help you get that appointment. I can get it for you. But we'll have to be more careful than we've been till the Governor makes his announcement.'

'You must forgive me, Sarita. About tonight. Seema

and I — well, we're taking a trip. I promise you. It won't be much longer. But I can't see you till I get back.'

'Kamal, I don't know if I like this or not.'

'Sarita, you've got to trust me.' The telephone receiver was sweat slicked now.

Her voice got throaty. 'I don't trust you. I never have. That's what makes you so exciting to me. I don't think I ever will trust you.' Her voice ran like gobs of hot chocolate. 'But when I get you — I won't let you out of my sight.'

I replaced the receiver and stood there, shivering. I looked at my watch. I wiped the sweat from my face. I started about the darkened house, feeling trapped.

Then I walked out of the house, got into the Fiat and drove like mad. I crossed the State line going north, just before daybreak.

WHAT DOES it feel like driving on a highway with a corpse in the back seat? You have got to experience it to feel. It can be hell.

I drove steadily, watching for every traffic sign and obeying them all. If a speed maximum called for 40, I stayed at an even 35, taking no chances on an eager patrolman.

I watched the rear mirror. Everything depended on how little attention I attracted in the next 48 hours — not so much on whether I got away with this part of the business, as to what would happen to me later.

My hands tightened on the wheel. This was the biggest part of the gamble, and yet I was not as worried about this moment as the days that must follow when I got away with this. If I did.

I could relax about what I was doing right now. Either I succeeded now, or the whole plan was shot and I was on the way to the gallows.

The bright glare of the morning sun was painful to the eyes, which burned from lack of sleep. I kept wiping at them with the back of my hand.

I could not keep my thoughts away from Sarita's call. What an impossible thing, and yet I knew I could have had that judgeship. I could have had it. In the rear mirror, I stared for a moment at Seema's placid face. I looked at her till my eyes became misty.

I jerked my gaze back to the highway. It was much more crowded now. Cars raced past me. Suddenly loud, and then the silence that followed when they pulled away. I was completely alone. Completely cut off from communication with any of those people. I was alone on earth. Alone with my thoughts — and with Seema.

There had never been a moment since my first year at high school when I had decided on law as a career that I had not dreamed myself into a judge's chair, bringing a new wisdom and fairness to it. And then in the chambers of the Supreme Court.

Kamalakar Sharma, a murderer.

My head was splitting. I passed restaurants, drive-ins, truck stops. All of them advertised the best food on the road. I glanced back at Seema, at that placid look on her face. I did not stop.

On the seat beside me was the pad and the pencil. Before I pulled out of the house, I had carefully noted the mileage. I had been driving about seven hours now. I still had one third of a tank of petrol. I told myself this was a good omen. It was a stroke of luck. The little car gave excellent mileage.

I did not stop for lunch. By 2 P.M., I knew I shall have to have petrol. This was the test. I had driven almost 700 kilometres; I had about 1,200 more to go. I swung off the north bound highway, on to a broad artery stretching east. I slowed, pulled off my jacket and lovingly covered Seema, tucking it about her throat and shoulders. She looked as if she were asleep. I could even believe it. The smile on her face was almost smug.

Sweating, I pulled into a petrol pump.

'Yes, sir?'

'Fill it up,' I said, keeping my voice low.

He glanced over my shoulder. He lowered his voice and grinned, 'Really sleeping, isn't she?

'Yes, we've been driving a long way.'

'See you people are from Bihar. Been down South?'

'Yes.'

He went back to the pumps, turned on the petrol and then checked under the hood. I watched him, feeling the sweat break out over my face. I felt greasy.

I looked around helplessly. It was as if that petrol hose chained me to this station. As though any moment that boy was going to realise that Seema would not remain asleep with the noise of the cars, the hood slamming down, the voices of the other attendants.

My gaze struck a pyramid of red cans of petrol. I stared at them a moment. Then I got out. I walked over and picked up one. I brought it back to the pump island where the attendant was just removing the hose from my tank.

'Will you fill this up for me?' I said. 'We want to try to make it home by tomorrow night. Maybe I won't be able to find a petrol station open late tonight.'

The boy shrugged. 'So many petrol pumps on the way, sir. Most of them are open all night — no trouble at all.'

I bit at the anger that welled in my mouth. I said, 'I don't know. Tired as I am. I may have to stop for a while.'

He was filling the can for me.

'Your wife doesn't drive?'

'No.'

He stared at me. 'You look very tired.'

IN ORISSA THAT NIGHT, my headlights picked out the name of the creek I was crossing. I saw that I was alone on the dark highway. I stopped, backed up.

I got out of the car, fatigue making my knees sink. I walked around a little to get some fresh air and to stretch out my legs. Far down the road behind me, I saw the pinpoints of head lamps. I ran back to my car, got in and drove away.

The highway wavered in front of me. It was early morning and the darkness pressed against the car windows. My eyes were heavy and dry, and felt scaly.

I awoke suddenly when my front tyre struck the shoulder on the left side of the highway.

I twisted the wheel and pulled back on the road. Behind me I saw headlights. If it was a State highway petrol, they would stop me for drunken driving. For the next few miles, I was wide awake. My head ached and I was feeling carsick. A horn was blaring behind me. I forced my eyes open. I was on the wrong side of the road. The horn went on blaring even when I pulled back on the right side.

I slowed down, so fatigued I did not care. If it was the police, at least it was all over.

A man leaned out of the window of the car when it pulled up beside me.

He yelled. 'You better have a cup of tea friend. Or else you're going to kill yourself or somebody else driving in your sleep.'

It was almost five in the morning and bitterly cold. The morning star shone brightly and there was a suspicion of grey on the eastern horizon. I stopped my car in the darkness and glanced at Seema.

I made for the dimly lit tea stall. A couple of peasants wrapped in blankets were warming their hands by a fire. An elderly Sikh, his beard loose, his turban off, sat on his haunches with his eyes fixed on a saucepan.

'*Sat Sri Akal.*' I greeted the Sikh.

'*Sat Sri Akal,*' he replied. He looked up from the saucepan and seemed pleased.

I ordered tea.

'*Bhai,* you look like you've been running all night,' remarked one of the peasants with a thick walrus moustache.

'Yes. I've been driving a long time.'

The Sikh bought me a tumbler of tea made of pure milk. I drank up the whole glass. The steaming tea soothed my nerves, and I felt better.

A uniformed policeman came. I held my breath. He looked around and smiled at the Sardarji. 'Who owns the black Fiat out there?' He waited. I did not speak, because I could not. 'Bihar licence,' he added.

'That's mine.' My voice croaked.

'You left your lights on. You won't have any battery.'

'Oh? Thanks.' I felt my shoulders sag. 'I was just going.'

The Sardarji laughed. 'Don't mind him. He's trying to set an endurance driving record of some kind.' My fists knotted. The last thing I wanted was to attract attention of any kind. The policeman was staring at me. I wanted to yell. I had been so careful right through the highway, and now I pulled into a tea shop and everybody in the place was looking at me.

'You better pull into a rest house somewhere and get some sleep mister,' the policeman said. 'You look like you need it.'

'Yes,' I said. 'I'm tired.' I handed over the money for the tea to the Sardarji and got out.

Just before dawn, I stopped beside a creek. I splashed some water on my face, then filled the petrol tank from the red can. I ascertained the mileage. I was getting over 40 kilometres per litre. I opened the bonnet. The water was cool and had not gone down even half an inch. It had not used any oil, either.

Very careful driver, I thought bitterly as I threw the empty petrol can into the creek and stood watching it float away.

Just as the sun was coming over the rim of the range of hills, I drove through a village clustered with mud huts. Partridges were calling in the tall grass. Peafowl were in the fields. I stopped the car and inquired from a passer-by the exact distance to Patna. He looked curiously at Seema in the back seat.

I had still 600 kilometres to cover.

I drove all day and when I reached Patna city, it was almost dusk. I drove through the city dodging pedestrians, cyclists, tongas and dogs. Soon I found myself on the national highway and I was approaching a small town. My headlights picked out the name of the town — Bukhtiarpur. Finally, I wondered how it had got its name. I drove on for a few kilometres past the town. I saw that I was alone on the dark highway. I pulled off the road into an unfenced wheat field. I made no attempt to conceal the car more than the darkness concealed it.

I stopped, turned off the engine, sat in the silence for a moment. Cars passed infrequently on the highway, their headlights small. At last, I gathered the strength to move. I wiped the car as clean as I could of fingerprints, consciously remembering every place I had touched it, even the hood and the water cap. I knew that fingerprints were useless unless made on a flat, smooth surface.

I left the keys in the ignition. I bent under the dashboard and using the screwdriver cracked two of the tubes in the radio.

I walked round the car, checking everything. Finally satisfied, I lifted Seema, finding her rigid and awkward. I placed her on the front seat, under the steering wheel and let her topple over.

Good-bye, Seema. This time it is really good-bye.

I slammed the car door and walked towards Bukhtiarpur. The stubbled wheat fields were dry, hardpacked. I did not even leave a footprint for them to trace.

I jogged along, every step seeming to vibrate against the top of my head. I stayed in the fields, walked around the town, crossed the railway tracks and at last reached the bus station. The last bus to Patna was about to take off. I got on the bus, found a seat and stumbled into it. The other passengers looked at me curiously. I fell asleep almost at once and did not hear anything else till the bus pulled into the bus station at Patna.

I WALKED along the main street of Patna, feeling better in the chilled air. I inquired from a passer-by about a good hotel. It was only a furlong away. I checked into an air-conditioned room. The moment my head touched the pillow, I was dead asleep.

Next morning, I awoke fully rested. I had an early breakfast and stepped out on the main road. I stopped at a barber shop, got a shave, haircut, shine and manicure. In an exclusive men's shop, I bought underthings, a shirt and a brown suit. I had them wrap up my old clothes and in the taxi, I removed the tailor's label from my old jacket. There were dry cleaners' symbols on my trouser pocket linings. But I did not think they would mean anything here, in Bihar.

In the taxi, I rode to the local Salvation Army. I handed them the bundle of clothes. I thought I carried it off well. 'My wife says if I don't get rid of this old suit, she'll get rid of me,' I smiled as I spoke.

It was getting easier. Better. I was beginning to think about Pushpa, wanting her.

AT THE AIRPORT, I bought a ticket for Bombay. When the Indian Airlines clerk asked my name, I gave him a blank smile. What the hell, I thought.

'Judge Dinanath Kapur,' I told him.

On the plane, I dozed off for a while, but I was restless. I awoke suddenly. I was going to be all right, I told myself. As soon as I saw Pushpa again, I would be all right. I dozed off again.

We had been in the air about an hour. Suddenly, I awoke again and shaken. Sure, I had yelled. Trembling, I looked around. Nobody was paying any attention. I sank back, breathing through my mouth.

I could not escape the dream. I had been sure Seema was sitting here beside me, stretched out so I was crowded against the bulkhead.

I asked the air-hostess for a newspaper. She gave me a copy of *The Searchlight*, a Patna newspaper. Of course, there was no mention of Seema's body having been found. How can the finding of a woman's body be news when the woman may have been driving alone and died of natural causes?

You might think the whole plan sounds amateurish and complicated. Full of unnecessary risk. You might say a lawyer with 15 years' practice ought to be smarter. But that was my angle. Sometimes, you can be too smart, you can outsmart yourself. And as I had told Pushpa, I wanted nothing to do with courts, insurance companies, or even with the police.

I wanted no risk. I had gambled all at once on that drive north, and I figured that car sitting out on the Bihar plains was going to give the police and the CID — a haemorrhage — a woman without identity, a car that belonged nowhere, dust from various States. They would be running round in circles, talking to themselves.

But I gambled that the circles would never widen to include Bangalore, about 2,000 kilometres South, or that they would even talk loud enough so the police in my community would overhear them. Sure, it was a complicated gimmick I was attempting. But if it kept me out of the police courts, that was what I wanted. When they tried to trace these clothes, that numberplate, or the stolen car, or even Seema herself — I was going to get away with murder.

All I wanted now was Pushpa.

I PHONED her as I reached Bombay. This time I did not stay at the Nataraj. I selected another hotel. My heart missed a beat when I heard her voice.

'As soon as it's dark, Pushpa, I need you. Come over here.'

'Yes....' There was a long, charged silence. 'Kamal?'

'Yes?'

'Kamal, did you do it?'

'Yes.' My head was throbbing.

She did not answer. I heard her breathing, fast and deep above the hum of the wires. At last she replaced the receiver, very gently and the connection was broken.

'IT'S DONE, Pushpa. That's all that matters. I don't want to talk about it. All I wanted was to get here to you, so I wouldn't have to think about it.'

She stirred on the bed, her eyes wide. 'Was it so bad, Kamal?'

I could not keep it in any more. Talk gushed out, bitterness underlining every word. I felt vile and I knew I would never get the vileness out of me. I told her how it was, how sick I had been after I knew Seema was dead. The living hell of driving 2,000 kilometres with a dead body on the back seat.

She moved closer. Her breath was hot against my face. I felt her body, her hands, her lips, but it was as if I had been hungry too long, and now I had no taste for anything. The more I tried to respond to her, the worse it became. My head throbbed so terribly, I thought my eyes would burst out of their sockets.

We had meals served in the room. We did not leave the room all night. I could forget everything, because I could have had what I wanted with Pushpa. The agony was that I could not make love to her.

'We must be careful, Pushpa.'

'I don't want to be careful. We can be together now, Kamal.'

'No. Not till we're married.'

She pressed her mouth against mine, soft and warm, fragrance of her breath on my face. 'It's over. She's dead and it's over.'

I stood up, not because I wanted to, but because I was afraid I would begin to believe her. Not till I'm sure I'm absolutely unsuspected.' She leaned forward on the bed, watching me. Her dark eyes gleamed. 'Will you ever know that, Kamal?' Her voice made me shiver. All my own doubts were in it.

From my pocket I took a letter Seema had written and gave it to Pushpa. 'I want you to imitate Seema's handwriting, Pushpa. As closely as possible. You must write a letter back home to Seema's best friend. Tell her that you — Seema — and I have fought and that you've applied for divorce. Tell her you plan to take a short holiday away from everything.'

'Will my handwriting fool Seema's best friend.?'

'Maybe she hasn't seen too much of it. Anyway you're supposed to be upset. Don't be careful with it. Scrawl your letters as though you're emotionally distraught. I don't care how you get it done, just so Manjari receives this letter.

Pushpa reached out for me. 'Kamal, I don't want you to leave me. I'm afraid when you're gone.'

I pressed my fists against my aching temples. 'So am I,' I said, 'but it's going to end, Pushpa, and we'll have each other.'

She sprang from the bed and pressed herself into my arms. She moved her mouth on mine and I felt better, as if it was worth it. It was all right as long as Pushpa was close against me.

Before I caught my train to Bangalore at Victoria Terminus, I bought the Patna newspapers from Higginbothams. On the train, I read the papers although my eyes seemed to bulge with the pain behind them.

I found it.

The Indian Nation had carried a short column. At first the Bihar State Police had thought the woman found in the car had died of a heart attack, but the doctors said she had suffocated. This puzzled the police who advanced the theory, she may have died from gas fumes, before she could get the engine off. Because the car had a Bihar number-plate, a photo of the dead woman had been taken. Foul play was suspected, and the CID had been called in.

I read till I could not read any more. I could see the fix they were in — a number-plate that did not belong to the car, a car that belonged to nobody, Seema's fingerprints useless, because they were on file nowhere.

I wadded up the papers and dropped them on the floor. I took two aspirins, but my headache stayed with me.

When the train pulled into Bangalore, I went first to the public telephone booth and phoned Sarita Shah.

'Seema has left me,' I told her.

'I'm bleeding.'

'I didn't expect you'd care, Sarita. I just thought you'd want to know.'

She laughed. 'Oh, you do want that judgeship, don't you, Kamal?'

'I'm sorry I called you.'

'Wait a minute, Kamal. Sorry I needled you. But I can tell you there's no appointment made yet. Don't you want me to come down and pick you up?'

'We've got to be careful.'

'Oh, Kamal. Not that careful. You wait in the station.'

I wanted to yell at her. I did not see how I could endure being in the same room with Sarita. My head throbbed. What could I say? I wanted that judgeship. It was the most important thing left to me now. 'All right, Sarita,' I said.

I had four more aspirins at Sarita's place. She stroked my face till I had to touch it to be sure, she had not worn a groove in it.

The sweet smell of the room was tormenting. My throat ached. I could feel how Seema must have felt with that pillow choking out her life.

As I was entering my house, I saw Mr Sarkar leaving for his office. Manjari Sarkar was with him, as he walked to the car. When she saw me, she came around the hedge and met me in the walk in front of the house. She looked worried. 'Kamal, what's the matter? Where's Seema?'

It was not hard to look distraught the way my head was aching. 'I may as well tell you, Manjari. You know Seema and I hadn't been getting along for months....'

'It was your fault, Kamal. Oh, I never knew anyone as crazy about her husband as Seema was.'

'Well, she left me, anyhow.'

'Kamal, I don't believe it.'

'It's true. It just didn't work out. We argued. When she left me she said she was going to Bombay. Well, I've this case coming up in court. I had to get back home. I couldn't run after her. Maybe she'll come to her senses.'

Manjari's face was grey. 'You have sense, Kamal. Get this silly case postponed and fly down to Bombay. And bring Seema home.'

'I couldn't do that.'

'Why not?'

'I went on this trip with her — when I couldn't afford the time. I did everything I could.'

Her head tilted. 'I don't think so, Kamal. You just rushed her out of the house in the middle of the night. She didn't ever get to buy any of the things she wanted to take.'

'I did the best I could.' The whole street was spining, and my eyes felt as though they were going to fall out.

'I don't think you ever really tried, Kamal. Not ever.'

A week later, I got a notice from the lawyer Pushpa had hired in Bombay. Seema was suing me for divorce, charging cruelty.

That morning *The Deccan Herald* carried a small item about it.

LOCAL LAWYER SUED

Kamalakar Sharma, well-known lawyer and young social leader of Bangalore, and his wife Seema have separated. Mrs Seema Sharma, prominent in local affairs, filed a suit for divorce in Bombay, charging cruelty. The couple has been married 18 years. There are no children.

I wrote to the lawyer advising him that I would not be in Bombay, and did not intend to contest the divorce.

I began to hate the house. I hated its stillness. I did not want to stay in it. I could not walk into the room where Seema had been killed. The housekeeper made up the bed and I closed the door and left it closed.

I was standing out on the sun porch when Manjari Sarkar came through the hedge at the place she and Seema had hacked out to make visiting back and forth easier.

When she came through the door, I saw she had a letter in her hand. I became more tense. This was the letter I had told Pushpa to write from Bombay. A lot would depend on how Manjari Sarkar reacted to that letter. Her face was drawn. She made no efforts to conceal her dislike for me. 'I have a letter from Bombay...' She paused. My heart thumped and then slowed. I felt the blood seep down from my face. 'It's from Seema.'

'Oh?' I started out across the yard, pretending it did not matter, yet afraid to let her see my face.

'Yes. It's a strange letter, Kamal. Doesn't sound like Seema.'

'What does Seema sound like?'

'Are you so bitter, Kamal? If there's any divorce, it's your fault. All your fault.'

'Oh, it's easy to pass judgement Manjari, when you don't know all the facts.'

'I don't say Seema was perfect. But she loved you. She'd have done anything to keep her home with you.'

'Maybe she was finally convinced, Manjari, that it was no good.'

'I didn't come here to argue with you. I have nothing to say to you, Kamal. I have said all I have to say. If Seema's in Bombay ...'

'Didn't you get a letter from her from up there?'

'... You better fly up there and get her back. I wouldn't have come here at all. But I wanted to see something that Seema wrote.'

I jerked my head around. 'Why?'

She had socked that one to me hard. I knew what was coming next. I held on tightly. And it came. 'I want to compare her writing with this letter. It seems so odd. Not like Seema.'

'For heaven's sake, what's the matter with you?'

'Nothing. Isn't there a letter here from Seema, or something she wrote?'

'Not that I know of, off hand.'

'Hasn't she written to you?'

'Why should she?'

She stared at me for a long time. At last she shook her head. 'I wish I could find something — this writing is all wrong.'

'Maybe Seema was upset. What do you want, Manjari? What are you trying to say?'

She shrugged. 'I don't know....'

'If you think something's wrong, tell me.'

'It's nothing, Kamal.' She backed away to the door.

'It's just that everything's so strange. Seema going away with you from here, not taking any of the things she planned to take. Then deciding to get a divorce when she has told me a hundred times she'd never get one. And this letter, that doesn't sound like her at all. And saying she's depressed and almost considering suicide.....'

'Oh?'

'Doesn't that sound funny to you? Seema's not chicken-hearted. She has never mentioned suicide to me before.

And what's more, if she's that depressed, she'd want to be with all her friends so they could help her.'

I stared at her. 'Maybe she finally figured her friends have helped her too much now — running to her with every lie they could think up.'

She laughed. She pushed the door open. 'Don't sound wounded, Kamal. It's all out of character. The dashing young lawyer, too damned good for little Seema. And now you don't even care that she's so unhappy.'

She walked across the yard, the letter still gripped in her hand. I stood there cursing her under my breath.

That evening I was in the front room. I had almost convinced myself that it would not look strange for me to close up this house and move to a hotel. One thing, I would be away from Manjari Sarkar, and her sixth sense, when all her other five were so poor.

The doorbell rang. I glanced at the windows, saw it was dark. I was afraid it was Sarita Shah. Things had been very quiet for the past few days between her and me.

It was Inspector Govinda Raju.

I knew at that moment what the rest of my life was going to be. It did not make any difference if I were suspected, or if I got away with it completely. That was what made it unbearable. I would never know when that knock would come, and some man would be standing there, the man with all the answers.

'May I come in, Counsellor?'

'Sure. Why not?' I stepped aside, leaning slightly against the door jamb. He walked past me.

'I won't beat around the bush with you, Counsellor.' He looked around the room. 'I read in the paper about you and the wife getting a divorce. Read that she was in Bombay. So we don't take this thing very seriously.' He swallowed hard. I offered him a drink and watched him shake his head.

'What thing?'

He lifted his shoulders. 'Oh. We got a letter down at headquarters. From Anonymous.'

'He's still writing letters?' I was afraid to lift the whiskey bottle. My hand was trembling. I straightened, shoved the hand in my pocket.

'Anonymous will be writing letters long after you and I are dead, Counsellor.'

'I guess so. What's the trouble now?'

'Seems it's very odd about your wife leaving home like this. We should investigate.'

Feeling slightly better, I showed him the divorce action. 'Well, that takes care of that. We'll check, of course,' he said. 'Has she written you any letters since she went away?'

'No. I didn't expect her to.'

'Odd. She didn't need any money —'

'She has her own. A hell of a lot more than I do.'

'I see.'

'She wrote a letter to the woman next door.'

'Oh? Fine. I'll check on that. That ought to clear it up.'

'Yes. As a matter of fact, Mrs Sarkar thought the letter sounded odd. I told her it was probably because Seema was upset. After all married 18 years...'

'Yeah, what sounded odd?'

'Nothing that I could see. But Mrs Sarkar thought Seema sounded very depressed.'

'Seem odd to you?'

'No.'

'Could it be that Mrs Sharma couldn't face the scandal here in town?'

'What scandal?' I felt as if he had hit me.

'Oh come now, Counsellor. Anonymous knew all about this. Seems you've been chasing a woman named Sarita Shah.'

'Good God. She's just a friend. She was a client of mine.'

'I'll check on that too,' he shrugged. 'I hope you understand, Counsellor. We're just checking. We've got no axe to grind. We feel nothing — yes or no. But we get these letters. Might be cranks. Might not. We check.'

'All right with me if you haven't anything better to do.'

'It's for you, just as much as against you, Counsellor. You see that.'

'Whatever you say. Sure you won't have a drink?'

'Not this time. When we meet again.'

'You mean I'll have to see you again?' I tried to laugh. So did he.

'Might. Who knows?'

PUSHPA WAS BACK at the office next morning. I could not wait to get there to see her. I had known she was flying in at night. But I did not dare to go near the airport. I sat by the phone. But I did not have the guts to call her.

I had promised myself I had taken care of all the angles. But suddenly I feared gossip. The publicity about the divorce was not going to help me get Narayan Prasad's job. I would have to do everything I could to counteract that. I was afraid to be seen chasing my secretary, or even displaying an interest in her.

She was in the reception room. I should grab her in my arms, welcome her home. She was in this all the way — an accessory to the deed. But I was on guard even against my deepest emotions.

Pushpa was too excited to notice my preoccupation. She locked the outer door when I entered. Finally, when she pulled away from me, I saw the agony in her eyes. 'We must talk, Kamal.'

'We've got to be careful, too. Till it's all over.'

'Why do we wait, Kamal? Why don't we just run away? Tell people you're going to Europe or the States. You've that much money. I'll meet you there. We'd never have to come back.'

She had dark rings under her eyes and seemed to have lost weight. 'What's the matter, Pushpa?'

'Nothing, Kamal. It's just we're taking chances we don't have to take. We can get out of the country now. Go somewhere where we can't be extradited.'

'I don't want such a place. I want that fifty lakhs. I want to get away with this.'

Her mouth quivered. 'But if you can't?'

'I can. I'm going to stay here. It may be rough. But I've got to win. There's a chance I may be appointed as District judge.'

'Kamal — you wouldn't accept that post.'

'Why wouldn't I? I'm going to. I'll sweat it out.' I tried to laugh. 'We've got these few minutes anyhow. Come here, darling.' I pulled her into my arms.

IT SEEMED she was gone again almost at once and I was alone. I paced my office. I sat down. I could not concentrate and started pacing again.

For the little while she was with me, it was all right. Then she had to return to Bombay, to pursue the divorce case and to write the second letter, which was the more important one. When she was with me time had raced the way a roller coaster does down a sharp incline. This time when Pushpa had been with me, she was more tense than ever. I was on edge too. I told her I was going to be judge Kamalakar Sharma. Nothing was going to stop me.

She cried for a long time before she left. I told her if I were to capitulate to her fears, I would have given into my own long ago.

I poured myself another whiskey. I had already finished half a bottle, but it was like drinking water. I could not rid myself of the tension. That was the worst of it. Not knowing what they were doing about Seema and the stolen Fiat out in Bihar. I wanted to be mentally at rest. Just so I could get an hour of peaceful sleep. I wanted to know what kind of inquiries the Government was making about me for the judge's post. I told myself I had a good record. That I had nothing to worry about. There was nothing to do but wait.

The phone rang. I knew who was calling — Sarita Shah. I did not want to answer. The thought of her, in an aura of perfume, was stifling. She had an insatiable hunger. And she had me right, exactly where she wanted.

If I was not nice to her, if I did not play ball with her, she could say the wrong things to the Governor. And I would never get that judgeship. Suddenly it seemed I had killed for that job. And I had to have it, no matter what I had to do for Sarita Shah. Once I got that job I could drop her. And there was nothing she could do.

I picked up the receiver. It was Sarita all right. The fifth time she had called that day. 'Kamal, you must give me an answer. I've told you. I've reserved a suite at the Silver Sands at Mahabalipuram for the weekend. I'm not going up there and waiting for you. Either you are going to meet me there, or I'm going to cancel the reservation.' There was a long pause. 'I don't think you want me to cancel it, Kamal.'

'I told you I couldn't get away just now, Sarita. No matter how much I'd like to. I just can't do it.'

'I think you can. Nothing is more important right now than getting to see you. After all, Kamal, you started this, you know. You wanted me — you ran after me —'

'I still want you, Sarita.'

'Whether you do or you don't, I think I know what you do want. I think you are smart enough to know that I haven't got the mildest temper in the world.'

'All right. All right.' I did not care a damn if the helplessness showed in my tone. She would not care about that either. 'I'll meet you there.'

'Saturday, Kamal.'

I left the office at noon on Saturday. I carried the small suitcase that had become almost a part of my regulation gear since I had got involved with Sarita Shah, the ever hungry man-eater.

I WAS on the kerb waiting for a taxi when Sabapathy Naidu pulled up in front of me in his new Standard. I had the inexplicable feeling he had been waiting for me to come out of the building. I tried to tell myself that did not make sense, but I had not been able to forget that black Fiat Millicento.

'Where're you going, Counsellor?'

'Got to make it to a train,' I said.

'Get in. I'll run you to the station. It's always a pleasure to do you a favour.'

I got in. I stared straight ahead. He drove like a maniac. 'I thought we were quits on the favour, Sabapathy.'

'Little favours. They mean nothing. Right, Counsellor?'

'If you say so.'

He stepped hard on the gas, then suddenly released the pedal. 'Oh, by the way Counsellor, did you ever get in touch with that hot-car fellow?'

'Which one?'

'Oh, come on Counsellor. The one you fought 20 minutes with me to get his name and personal phone number. That one.'

'No.' I said. 'I changed my mind. Why?'

He chewed on his *pan*. 'Good thing, though you never phoned him. The CID found a car in Bihar. A Fiat. Traced it to a town up in Andhra Pradesh. What do you think of that, Counsellor? Pretty smart, those boys, eh?'

My fists clenched tight. He glanced at me a moment, looked back at the street just in time to swerve round a warehouse lorry.

'What sort of a car was it?'

'Who knows? Who cares? It doesn't affect us. There was a dead body in that car. Funniest thing. They came on to my friend. They got rough with him. Really worked him over.'

I was dumbfounded. There had to be more. But I could not ask. Sabapathy's face was taut, waiting for me to show some interest.

'Glad you never used the name and the number I gave you, Counsellor. Because I'd have been in a jam. I'd hate to have that fellow mad at me after he had a round with them CIDs.'

He swerved the car into the kerb in front of the station. 'This is it, Counsellor. Have a good time.'

I got out. Sabapathy Naidu stared at me a moment, and

then stepped on the gas. This was it. He knew a lot of things I had to know. And he was not going to tell me. This had to end. Because now it was just a race to see whether I or my perfect murder came unglued first.

I was shivering as though I had a chill by the time I got off the train in Madras. I stared at the Silver Sands Hotel station wagon and the other cars parked beside it. I thought how crazy it was. Once I had wanted people to see me when I was with Sarita Shah. Now I was sick at the thought that somebody might spot us together.

'Kamal. Kamal, darling. Over here.' Sarita was in a hired car. I forced myself to grin and walked over. Other weekend guests piled into the station wagon and the other cars. Sarita gave me a seductive smile and clung to me. Even after she moved away, the pungent perfume of her make-up remained in my nostrils.

We drove to the hotel. She told me I did not have to check in. She had done that for me. When a bellboy tried to take my bag, she tossed him a rupee and told him I was a big strong man. I could carry my own bag.

I tried to stall her into the lobby lounge for a drink, but she did not agree. She had thought of everything. When we were up in the room, and the cloying perfume was already beginning to suffocate me, she put her arms round me and pressed me to her. I felt a sudden revulsion that made me almost physically ill.

'Isn't this delightful?' she said.

'Sure.' I was wishing I knew what those CID men were doing out in Bihar.

She pressed against me harder, her body giving. 'Being alone in a hotel room with a man does crazy things to me, Kamal. I could hardly wait for you to get here.'

What was wrong with the bellboys? I thought. She was

crowding me. I could hardly breathe even with the windows open, and the breeze pouring in.

'I thought you were annoyed with me.'

She was becoming more romantic. She began to undo her bra. I lay back. And I closed my eyes so I would not see her when she spilled from her bra. Maybe if I did not look at her, it would not be so bad, I thought.

'You sure don't act as if you really want me,' she said. One of the worst tortures yet devised for man is having to pretend ardour for a woman he despises.

'I'm here,' I said. 'Isn't that enough?'

'It's something,' she said. 'But not enough.'

We did not leave the rooms that weekend. She ordered our meals sent up. She would not even let me handle that little chore. She smiled and kept caressing me all the time. And kept telling me she wanted to do everything for me. She did not want me to move, except to love her. And that is just about the way it was.

My mouth felt raw when she covered it with her full lips. She ran her hands over me till they were like crawling ants. The cloying scent never receded for a moment. I had cabin fever, the way no man ever contracted before. And all that time, mixed up with her perfume and her hands and her mouth was the agony over what the police were doing.

She would not let me sleep. I suppose I could not have slept, anyway. But if only I could get away from her just long enough to stand at the window and get a breath of fresh air. It did not happen that way. She talked about how beautiful I was going to look as a judge. The things we were going to do when my divorce with Seema was final, and we no longer had to hide like this.

I had to get out of there. I thought I never would be able to. But Monday came. I talked Sarita out of accompanying me back to Bangalore, on the train. I told her unless she had positive knowledge I was not going to get that judge appointment, we had to make a pretense at respectability.

I got out of there before dawn. And caught the Brindavan Express back to Bangalore.

'BEEN AWAY, COUNSELLOR?' Govinda Raju eyed the suitcase, looking me over as I unlocked the door and told him to come in.

My mind was in a whirl. I was too depleted. I was sure that something had broken in Seema's murder. Something I had overlooked. Something I had forgotten. Rapidly I checked over everything. But I could not see where I had gone wrong. It was a perfect job as far as I was concerned.

I did not look at Govinda Raju. I could not trust myself to let him see the fear that must be showing in my eyes.

I walked straight to the water cooler. I ran a glass of water, feeling the glass chill against my fingers.

'Been doing some heavy drinking, Counsellor?'

'Why?' I spoke over my shoulder.

'Heavy drinking. And you need a lot of cold water the next morning.'

'No,' I said. 'It's just that I've been away. Nothing tastes so good as hometown water. Particularly when you've been away.'

He watched me drink.

'Where have you been?'

I had no idea what he was leading up to. How much he knew. Or why he was waiting for me. 'Just a little business trip,' I said.

'Oh yeah. But do you mind saying where?'

I still wanted that judgeship. I was not going to jeopardize it till I found out what was on his mind. 'New Delhi,' I said. 'I flew down.'

His brow tilted. But after a moment he shrugged. He leaned against the desk watching me. His voice was low. 'I guess you haven't heard, then.'

'No. Heard what?'

'Your wife.'

Somebody had pulled the world from under me. I wanted to sit down before I fell.

'Seema?' I whispered it at him.

'You look bad, Counsellor. Why don't you sit down?' That soft tone had not changed. But this did not go with his jut jawed coldness. I sat down on the reception room couch. All right, Govinda Raju, I thought. Let us get it over with.

'What about Seema?'

'She's been murdered, Mr Sharma. I hate to be the, one to tell you. We just got word. It was brutal.'

'Brutal?' My head jerked up. 'Seema?'

'Yes Sir. We just got word from the police from Bombay. Somebody beat her to death.'

I looked at him a moment. And he began to sail slowly. He was moving in a grey arc before my head. I opened my mouth. I tried to speak. But there was no words. And I crumpled forward on the floor, passed out cold.

I CAME out of it slowly. The reluctance to start living again was the strongest urge in me. Govinda Raju kept waving smelling salts under my nose till I sat up and moved away from it.

'Take it easy, Mr Sharma.'

Take it easy. Pushpa was dead. Pushpa. Somebody had killed Pushpa. Beaten to death.

I turned my head in my hands. It did not make sense. It wheeled around in my brain. And did not make sense at all. Sure. Govinda Raju said Seema. The police wired from Bombay that it was Seema. Why not? Wasn't Pushpa registered up there as Mrs Kamalakar Sharma. Govinda Raju showed me the *Deccan Herald*. And they had printed Seema's picture with the wire service story from Bombay. That morning in the hotel room Mrs Kamalakar Sharma brutally slain, police seeking unknown assailants.

I hunched there reading the story. They had printed the life sketch of Seema. Her birth, marriage, clubs, social activities, all the local stuff.

I kept swallowing the sickness that gorged up in my throat. I thought about the judgeship, and I knew it was gone. But that did not seem very important. The police had only the first instalment of the story, which was all twisted. Wait till they started to dig. Wait till they found out that was not Seema at all. That it was Pushpa posing as Seema, getting a divorce from me in Seema's name. I shuddered. I refused to think any further.

'Mr Sharma?'

I was trembling. I looked up. I was startled to see pity in Govinda Raju's brown eyes. I looked away quickly.

'Why don't you let me take you home Mr Sharma? Nothing we can do around here.'

I glanced at the wilted flowers in the vase on Pushpa's desk. I shivered. Pushpa was dead. Up in Bombay, Pushpa was dead. I remembered suddenly that she was nervous and upset while she was here, in Bangalore. She had wanted me to take her away. Out of the country. She had kept talking about going before it was too, late.

Well, now it was really too late!

We drove through town on Govinda Raju's motorbicycle. I tried to look at the town, the buildings and trees and people as we passed. But they had no reality.

'Bombay Police want you to go up there.'

'No.' The word burst out of me.

He glanced at me, scowling. 'They need you, Mr Sharma. It's murder. One thing, they'll expect you to identify the body.'

I did not speak.

'Another thing, they'll expect you to cooperate on is, who might have hated your wife enough to kill her like that.'

'I don't know.'

'You think about it, Mr Sharma. This is a bad crime. I know you and your wife were not hitting it off so well. And she was up there getting a divorce. This is a killing. And the police are going to need your help to find that killer.'

'I don't know what I could tell them.'

'We can talk it over.'

'We?'

'Yeah. Police want me to fly up there with you. I told them. Well. I said you were a friend of mine. And I would be glad to go along with you. I want to help you, Mr Sharma. I know we have seen eye to toe on a lot of things. But when a man is in trouble like this...'

I swallowed back the sickness, thinking, if you only knew.

'There's one thing,' he said. His voice had a regretful tone as though he disliked bringing it up just now.

'Yeah?'

'That trip you took.'

I swallowed back the sickness again. It was more difficult.

'Yes.'

'New Delhi.'

I did not answer. He glanced at me.

'You say you flew? I hope there was somebody that you know that might have seen you.'

'What are you talking about?' I knew what he was talking about, all right.

'I hate to say it, Mr Sharma. But I might as well. Then Bombay Police will certainly say it. You might as well be ready for them. Now on this flight to New Delhi you see anybody you knew? A man could fly from here to Bombay and back over Sunday, Mr Sharma. Then Bombay Police are sure going to think that. So if there's somebody that can say you were really in New Delhi, you better get in touch with them right away.'

We moved through the streets for what seemed a long time without speaking. My mind was racing. I kept thinking I might as well give up. It was just a matter of time now. The trap had been sprung — and not from Bihar at all. But from Bombay. There would be no appointment to a judge's bench now. There would be none of Seema's money. I could not see what would be left. I felt as though some things were crawling all over my body. All I could think was that, maybe, somehow I could save my skin.

I was down to that now.

'Well, Mr Sharma, how about it? You able to think of anybody?'

'I know somebody...'

'Yeah.'

'This person can swear I wasn't in Bombay over the weekend.'

'That's fine.'

'But I — well — I lied to you.' I felt a chill all over my body.

'Yeah. What about?'

'About New Delhi. I didn't exactly go to New Delhi. I didn't fly.'

'No. Where were you?'

'I was in Mahabalipuram.'

'The whole weekend?'

'That's right. From Saturday till early this morning.'

'You got somebody can swear to that?'

'Yes ...Sarita Shah.'

That cut it. Whatever pity I had seen in his eyes was gone. His mouth was a tight line. He was a policeman again, all policeman, and I was on the other side of the high wall.

THREE MORE POLICEMEN arrived at the house. One was a Police Inspector and the other two were Sub-Inspectors.

'Sir,' one of the Sub-Inspectors said to Govinda Raju. 'Just got some airmailed pictures here from up in Bombay. Something is funny.'

This policeman had glossy photos in his fist. I stared at them as if I could never pull my gaze away. But I did not have to see them to know what they were. The way the sun hit them they still appeared fresh from the developing solution. They were that new. But to me they were already old.

Govinda Raju reached for the photos.

The policeman surrendered them and then they crowded each side of Govinda Raju looking at them as if they had never seen them before. They did not even remember me. But it did not matter. My legs were tired. I did not move.

Finally, Govinda Raju turned and looked at me. His jaw had receded slightly. And his eyes were wide.

'Mr Sharma.'

I just looked at him.

'There's really something funny. This woman isn't Mrs Sharma. She's dead, but she isn't Mrs Sharma at all.'

I still did not speak. I was too tired to pretend anything. I did not have to reach for it any more. They were slugging me with everything already.

'I know this woman,' Govinda Raju said. His voice sounded strange. 'It isn't Mrs Sharma. It's surely not Mrs Sharma — And yet it's somebody I know…' He stared at the pictures some more, shuffling them in his hands. Then he swung round and jerked his head at me. 'Here, Mr Sharma. Come, take a look at these.'

I walked woodenly and entered the circle formed by the policemen. One of the policemen made a place for me beside Govinda Raju. I glanced around, looking for something to lean against. There was nothing.

'Look at these pictures. Know this woman?'

They were the brutal, unblinking Police Lab pictures technicians take at the scene of the crime. They were not prettied up at all. Govinda Raju held each one before my face for what seemed an interminable time. In an instant, I saw more than what I wanted to see. More than I could take. Pushpa, I thought. My God! Poor, Pushpa!

I was afraid I was going to be sick. Govinda Raju bumped me with his shoulder. 'How about it, Mr Sharma? What you got to say. Who's this woman?'

I wanted to speak. There was no sense holding back

information like this from him now. The police at Bombay probably already knew the truth. Pushpa had only registered as Mrs Kamalakar Sharma. She had not carried the masquerade any further. It had not seemed necessary. There must have been personal belongings, or identification cards, marked with her real name. But it was hard to speak. It was taking one more step towards the gallows.

I licked at my lips. There was a barrier in my throat. And the words had to clear it.

'Come on, Mr Sharma. Speak up. You know this woman. She lives here in Bangalore. She works around here. Why, I've seen her recently. Oh, yeah. Sure. God Lord, don't you recognize her? She's your secretary.'

I nodded. It was not easy.

'Pushpa. Pushpa Rao. That's her name.' Govinda Raju said, scowling. He no longer expected anything from me.

'Then this isn't Mr Sharma's wife?' One of the policemen said.

'That's what they told us at Headquarters. But they say she sure is registered at the hotel as Mrs Kamalakar Sharma of Bangalore.'

Govinda Raju glanced at me. He spoke to one of the policemen. 'Make this man sit down, before he drops on to the floor.'

The policeman touched my arm and I moved like an automaton. 'Sit down there,' the policeman told me. He was a young fellow, about 25, with a hectic flush and nervous hands. Govinda Raju's voice had told him I was not due any deference. Earlier, I had been the bereaved husband. But now I might be the murderer. I stumbled and sank down on the sofa.

That is the way with trouble. It can never hit you fast enough or hard enough. The room spun oddly. I did not even look up when Govinda Raju crossed the room, snapped on the reading lamp beside my chair and tilted its shade so that the glare struck the side of my face.

'Look up,' Govinda Raju ordered.

I lifted my head. The light was painful in my eyes. I tried to lower them.

Govinda Raju's voice was sharp. 'I got a question I want to ask you. A big one.'

I stared up at him. I was groggy. Too groggy to think about the right I had always fought the police over with clients of mine. Right now I was no client. I was hanging on the ropes, reeling. I was not thinking. I was reduced to nothing.

'Now this secretary of yours. Pushpa Rao. Now we got the word from the police up in Bombay that this Rao woman has been posing as your wife up there for almost a couple of months. Part of that time she has been down here. I know. I've seen her in your office. She's dead. She has been murdered. But that's not what's troubling me. I want to know something else. I want a straight answer.'

'Yes.'

'Where's your wife, Sharma? Where's Seema Sharma?'

GOVINDA RAJU LEANED OVER ME. 'You better know. The Police Headquarters up in Bombay wants you, Mr Sharma. They want some explanations. We're going up there, but before we go we're straightening out the loose ends down here. You're trying to make fool out of some one, Sharma. But it's not going to be me.'

'I don't know — what you're talking about.'

'You don't have to know what I'm talking about. You're

going to sit right there and I'm going to hear it. It didn't mean much — without this murder — and these pictures. It didn't look good, of course. But it didn't add up to anything. I just took you for a fellow with hot pants who's playing around with one of his wife's friends.'

He stopped talking, his voice loud and cold in that silent house. The other uniformed policemen stood rigid, watching him.

'But now let's see what we've got? We start with a phone call from a nameless character — a letter from anonymous. He says your wife isn't in Bombay. He says that something is wrong and we ought to check.

'So I checked. You seemed convinced your wife was in Bombay. Told me about the letter Mrs Sarkar got. You want to hear about that letter? It was never written by your wife. No, Sir. I got the testimony of a graphology expert on that. Sure, I agreed with you. Poor Mrs Sharma. All upset. Didn't care how she wrote.

'Then Mrs Sarkar, she didn't think that letter came from your wife, either. Seems there was a lot of things your wife wanted to do before she left town. Yet she left without doing any of them. Without taking things she planned to take.

'So maybe your wife was never in Bombay at all. If she wasn't, what have we got? Looks like you and this Pushpa Rao were in on a murder — of your wife.'

I sat forward. 'You must be mad. I wouldn't dream of murdering my own wife. And it's Pushpa who's dead — not Seema.'

'All right. So maybe Seema's not dead. Where's she, Mr Sharma?'

'I don't know.'

'Where's your wife?'

'I told you, I don't know.'

'And I'm telling you. You better find out. We got a dead woman up there in Bombay. We also got you coming back from a weekend trip that you've lied about once — may be twice.'

'I told you how you could check that weekend.'

'And don't think I won't check. But what does it give us? Something else. Another motive for killing?'

'Why would I want to kill Pushpa Rao?'

'I don't know yet. But I'll find out. And now you're feeling better. The smart lawyer.'

'I'm smart enough to tell you to arrest me, or get off my back.'

'Technically, Sir, you are under arrest. Just let's not get away from our theme. I didn't say that you wanted to kill Pushpa Rao. That'll come later. I'm talking about why you would want to kill your wife.'

'Who said my wife was dead?' The words ripped out of me.

'You haven't said where she is.'

'I have told you. I don't know.'

'So maybe she's dead.'

'What're you driving at?'

'At you, mister. At a fellow running around with his wife's friend. And his wife? Broken-hearted. Enough so that friends will believe she's up in Bombay getting a divorce.'

'She said she was.'

'Oh, come now, Counsellor. You're smarter than that. There isn't even one Mrs Kamalakar Sharma up there in Bombay. And we got a picture of her. Dead. Pushpa Rao posing as your wife. Dead up there in Bombay. But that don't tell us where your wife is.'

'All right. Maybe she's not in Bombay.'

'Sure. Maybe she isn't. But she isn't up in Bombay. Where's she?'

'I don't know.'

'If she didn't write that letter saying she was up there in Bombay —'

'Who says she didn't?'

'I say she didn't. Experts say she didn't write that letter. So what do we do on that? We show them that letter again — only this time we let them compare it with the handwriting of your secretary. How about that, Mr Sharma? What do you think we'd get then?'

'I don't know. This is your pipe dream.'

'Yeah. You had your own dream, didn't you?'

'What dream?'

'Playing fast and loose with this Sarita Shah. Why not? What did your wife have except a lot of money? How much, Mr Sharma? And if she died, who'd get it?'

'Who said she died?'

'Nobody has told me anything about her. That's what I'm waiting for. Meantime, I'm telling you what it looks like to me. You hired this Pushpa Rao to go to Bombay and pose as your wife, and sue you for divorce. Had her write a phony letter to Seema's best friend. You planned to have her write another phony letter this time addressed to you, saying that she was committing suicide and you can keep all her money...'

'You have imagination, Inspector, some imagination.'

'And now all your planning is a fiasco.'

I did not answer. My eyes were watering from the glaring light. I could not speak. Govinda Raju had it as if he were reading from the mental script I had carefully prepared all these weeks, thinking I was clever, original and unbeatable. Sweat dropped along my ribs.

'Is that it Sharma? Is that the pattern?'

'I don't know what you're talking about. My secretary was killed in Bombay. Now you're accusing me of killing not only her, but my wife too. I told you I can prove where I was last weekend.'

'You're going to get a chance to do that.'

'Then arrest me, or drop it.'

'There's still the other little matter. Your wife. She wouldn't give you a divorce. Is that it, Mr Sharma? Loved you though you were such a dog. She loved so much you had to kill her to get rid of her.'

I was sweating.

'The woman who's dead,' I whispered to him, my voice hoarse and choking, 'is named Pushpa, Push... Pushpa.'

'Sure she is. But what I want to know is, where's Seema Sharma?'

The doorbell rang sharply. And Govinda Raju straightened, sighing.

'Swamy.' He spoke over his shoulder. 'See who that is at the door. And send him away, unless he knows where Seema Sharma is.' His laugh was sharp.

Swamy walked out of the room, and returned with two more uniformed police officers.

I stared at them blankly. I was too beaten now to care what news they brought.

'Govinda Raju.' They called him over and I sank back in the chair, pushed the light away. I watched them talking. And they were looking at a set of new pictures.

Finally, Govinda Raju spun on his heel and strode back over to me. His face was cold. And his jaw jutted.

'Up in Bombay they know more about this Rao woman than we do, Mr Sharma. But they don't know as much about you. As far as they know, you're a bereaved husband.

They don't know about Sarita Shah and your wife's money.'

'No more than you do.'

'I know plenty about you. But they're looking for another man.'

He watched my face for effect.

I stopped breathing. This did not have to hit me as hard as it did. I must have realized somebody beat Pushpa to death in her hotel room. The chances were that it was a man. But somehow, in the confusion, another man had not seemed real. A man who was intimate enough to be in her room early Sunday morning. The pictures of what she was wearing — that sheer negligee, which I had presented to her. It had to be a man who hated — or loved — Pushpa enough to kill her in passion and anger.

Another man. A lover. Pushpa's lover. I had to say it over and over to believe it. Even now.

My face must have told Govinda Raju plenty because he laughed. It was a contemptuous sound. 'What did I tell you, Counsellor. Years ago. If she'll step out with you, later, she'll step out on you. Every time, Counsellor.'

'I don't know what you're talking about.'

His voice was sharp. 'That is what I'm talking about. Those people at the Headquarters up in Bombay sent this picture because they thought Mr Sharma might know the man suspected of murdering Mrs Sharma. They don't know yet it isn't Mrs Sharma. But they do send word that she'd filed for divorce. Is that the divorce you sent Pushpa Rao up there to get, Mr Sharma?'

'I don't know what you're talking about.'

He laughed. 'So you flew up there Saturday, and spent the night with her?'

Now I laughed, a forced sound. 'They're looking for another man, remember?'

'Sure. They are. Because they don't know what we know. They say the neighbours said this man was with her all the time up there. And the hotel people say that he checked out suddenly Sunday morning and that he was using a phony name. 'What phony name did you use up there, Counsellor?'

'I told you I wasn't in Bombay.'

'I heard you. You got everything to win. This guy has nothing.' He leaned forward. He thrust a picture at me. I stared at it. I stared for a long time, because from the first instant it seemed familiar — waved hair, pencilled moustache, twisted smile.

'You know him, Mr Sharma?' Govinda Raju said. 'Somebody who was a friend of your secretary?'

I shook my head. 'I never saw him before.'

Then suddenly it came rushing over me. And I remembered this fellow. Sure. Why not? It was the fellow in the room across the corridor from Pushpa. The only one. When I asked her about him, what had she said? What a quaint expression? What an old-fashioned expression? Oh, my God. Neat. Changing the subject, without appearing to be interested. Her boy friend. The neighbours said they were together all the time! The gigolo. I saw the way he had stood there, saying he needed a cigarette, keeping me speared in that light from his room, while he looked me over, staring at me with that twisted smile on his face.

Suddenly that smile had a new meaning. It meant he knew me. He knew Pushpa. And he knew all about me. That is what that smile had been saying. Only I did not know.

WHAT COULD I tell Govinda Raju? That I had seen this man? Just once? In front of Pushpa Roa's room? No. How could I?

All I could do was think about Pushpa's begging me to leave the country. Begging me to leave with her while we still had a chance.

That night I killed Seema — the telephone rang and I could have had Narayan Prasad's post in the District and Session's bench. But it was just too late. An hour before the murder that telephone call might have changed everything. And then Pushpa had begged me to get out of the country — afraid to tell me about that man in Bombay.

Govinda Raju leaned over me. 'Listen to me. I want to know where your wife is.'

'Find her then.'

'I'll find her. Meanwhile, if I had my way, I'd jail you on just what I know.'

'What you think you know isn't just good enough, Govinda Raju?'

'Feel clever now, Counsellor? Oh God. The way you looked in your office when I told you your wife had been killed up therein Bombay. You looked so sick, I was sorry for you. Sorry for you! And all the time I was thinking how you were hit by the news of your wife's death. It wasn't at all that you knew it wasn't your wife. You knew your wife wasn't ever in Bombay. When I said Bombay, you knew it was your secretary who was dead.'

'If I'd known she was dead, I wouldn't have been shocked.'

'There are answers, and I'll have them. I'll have them all. When I get them, we can start shaving your head.'

The doorbell rang as Govinda Raju turned to walk away.

He glanced over his shoulder. 'Looks like another load of bad news for you.'

I stood up. Swami opened the front door. And I recognized Sarita Shah's sugary voice. I trembled. Govinda Raju had turned now and was laughing at me, his eyes cold and deadly.

Sarita walked into the room. I stared at her. I wondered how she could be such a fool. Had she not seen all those police vehicles out in front? Did she need an engraved invitation to get lost at a time like this? Did she not have sense enough to know that people had linked our names, and that she was helping me to the gallows?

Govinda Raju did not look at Sarita. He did not take his gaze off my face.

'Kamal.' She held out her arms and ran to me, ignoring the policemen. 'Poor Kamal. I came as quickly as I could. As soon as I heard. Poor Seema — murdered like that out in that far away place!'

Over her head, I saw the knowing glances. I tried to hold her away. 'Sarita there's something you ought to know...'

'Who could have done such a thing? Who, Kamal? Such a brutal thing! Poor Seema!'

Govinda Raju laughed. It was an ugly, brutal sound in the silent room. Sarita stepped back slightly. She stared at Govinda Raju. Her face was white.

'There's just a slight error, Mrs Shah...'

'How do you know my name?'

'I'm afraid there's a lot I know about you.'

She frowned. Her face was still white. And then she turned and looked at me.

Why the hell did she not stay at home, I thought.

'Kamal, what's it? What's the matter?'

Govinda Raju laughed again. 'It's just that you're mixed up, Mrs Shah. It wasn't his wife that was killed. At least not the one you read about in the papers. By the way, did you just get back in town?'

Her head tilted. She ignored his last question. 'But Seema's picture was in the morning paper. I saw it.'

'Yeah. But it was a mistake. It was not Mr Sharma's wife that got herself killed Sunday morning. It was his secretary. Pushpa Rao. You know her?'

Sarita's face went white. It was as if he had struck her. I felt weak and leaned against the arm of the chair. Sarita did not know Pushpa. That was clear enough in her shocked expression.

Govinda Raju stepped towards her, before she recovered. 'There's a question I'd like to ask you, Mrs Shah. It'll be a big help to Mr Sharma if you cooperate. He says he was with you over the weekend. Would you care to tell me whether that's true or not?'

All the indecision was gone from Sarita's face now. She glanced around the room, seeing the police actually for the first time, seeing what their presence meant. She looked Govinda Raju over slowly. He had played his trump card with her. He had let her know what he thought of her. And she was no longer awed by him, or afraid of him. All that was in the chilled glance she gave him. The sugary sweetness had disappeared from her tone. And I saw that Sarita was thinking fast.

Why did not she answer him? What did she expect to gain by refusing to answer?

'I won't answer,' she told him evenly.

'Sarita!' The word burst out of me. I could hear myself yelling that name despairingly as I walked down the corridor, towards the gallows.

'It's all right,' she said. 'I'm sure, Kamal, you'll agree. I don't have to answer any questions till I've talked to my lawyer.'

Govinda Raju laughed. 'Sharma is your lawyer, Sarita?'

'Yes, he is. I want to talk to him before I answer my questions that'll tend to degrade or incriminate me.'

He laughed again. 'There he is. Talk to him.'

She shook her head. 'Alone. I'm not going to talk to him in front of all these policemen.'

Govinda Raju seemed to be enjoying himself. He spoke to Swamy. 'Let them talk in that room there. Keep the door ajar. And stand where you can watch them.'

'I think you better start by telling me the truth,' Sarita said as soon as they were alone.

'I've told you the truth.'

'Kamal, you're in a bad spot. A very bad spot. It was bad enough when I thought it was Seema who was dead up there in Bombay.'

'You know I didn't kill Pushpa Rao. I was with you.'

'Yes. But there are too many things I don't know. In the first place, you told me on the phone before you ever left here with Seema that you were going to get a divorce. But all the talk I've heard since then was that Seema and you were on a trial second honeymoon that didn't work out, and that she left you and went to Bombay.'

'You know how rumours get around.'

'All right. I am willing to believe they were rumours. Because I know something that these people didn't know. I knew I held the aces. I had something you wanted. I believed you'd parted with Seema because I had what you couldn't get — not without me. You wanted to be a judge. I believed you were telling me the truth. Now I don't know.'

'Why should I lie to you?'

'Suppose you tell me the truth and let's find out. Why not start by telling me why Pushpa Rao was in Bombay, posing as your wife, getting a divorce in her name?'

'I don't know.'

'Kamal, you're smarter than this. I always thought you one of the smartest lawyers I know. Now you sound like a schoolboy caught in his first lie.'

'I swear I don't know who killed Pushpa Rao.'

Her voice lowered. 'Maybe we better clear up about Pushpa first.'

I felt myself go cold all over. I waited, watching her.

'I suspected you from that first day you met me at the Jewel Box, Kamal. I'd tried too long to get you. And you gave me the brush. Suddenly you were chasing me. There had to be a reason. I couldn't stand not knowing. So I found out you were dating your pretty little secretary. I had you followed, all those times when you were letting people believe you were with me.'

'Good Lord, Sarita!'

'You sound beat, Kamal. You had me right where you wanted me. Oh, you had me pegged. I was too vain. I'd never tell anybody the truth about where you really were. I should have hated you, Kamal, and I did. But I was intrigued, I know this was leading to something. You were using me. And I hated you for that too. But I wanted to see what you expected to gain. Your little secretary running off to Bombay — you following her — and all the time people were whispering that you were with me.'

'Why did you let me get away with it?'

'Oh Kamal, you don't sound like yourself at all. I told you, I was waiting. I wanted to see what you'd do. What you'd have the guts to do to me. Then Narayan Prasad died and I saw that no matter what your plans had been, I could change them. Oh, I had you pegged too, Kamal. Selfish, ambition-driven Kamalakar Sharma. You think I didn't know how you hated Seema because you couldn't get your hands on her fortune all at once? But you had many things I loved, Kamal, and I thought I could buy you. I could make you a judge. I could start you to where you wanted to fly.'

I did not say anything. I wiped the back of my hand across my mouth. My brain felt as if it had turned mush.

'So when you came back this time, I was sold, Kamal. Seema was getting a divorce. And you and I could be together, and I could get that appointment for you. But not now. A divorce scandal I could have handled. But murder — not even your wife, but your mistress. One of your mistresses. Your secretary, your secret love, up in Bombay, pretending to be your wife. I don't know now, Kamal. You want me to go in there and tell the police that you were with me all the weekend. Should I compromise myself for your future, after all that you've done to me?'

'Good Lord, Sarita. You've got to tell the truth.'

'Do I? Didn't you use me when it was a lie? I let people believe you were with me, when you weren't at all. You were in a hotel somewhere with Pushpa. You were in Bombay with Pushpa. Why should I tell them you were with me in Mahabalipuram, and hurt my reputation that much more? You saw what the police officer thought of me — a common strumpet, as far as he was concerned — because of what people have said about you and me. Should I make it worse? Let it get in the papers that you were with me for another romantic weekend in Mahabalipuram when you don't intend to marry me and never did.'

'Oh God. Sarita, you can't let me down!'

'No, Kamal. I can. I have let you use me for the last time — I get nothing out of it, but hurt.'

I caught her arm.

'Let me go, Kamal, you hurt me.'

'I've held you a lot harder than this.'

'But then I wanted you to,' she twisted.

'Sarita, it's still your word against mine. I told them I was with you. I had to.'

'Well, that's too bad. Because my word is better than yours. And I'll say you weren't with me.'

'You must be mad!'

'Am I? Then thank yourself, Kamal. I wasn't mad till you started using me for a wrestling bag.'

'The people in Mahabalipuram —'

She laughed in my face. 'Who saw you there, Kamal? A bellboy who won't remember. I registered as a single. I ordered all our meals in the room. Whom did you talk to? Kamal, who saw you there? Who really saw you well enough to swear that it was you — and not anyone else who resembled you. After all it could have been anybody.'

I stared around the room. Nothing looked substantial. I wished the floor might give way and let me sink forever downward But that would have been too good to happen. My voice shook.

'What do you want, Sarita?'

'What do you mean, what do I want?'

'You'll tell the truth. It's got a price. What's it?'

She smiled. 'That's better. I was happy when I thought I'd have you Kamal. I thought the judgeship would buy you. Now I can't offer you that...' She traced her fingers along my face. I shivered.

'All I can offer you now, Kamal, is an alibi that might save your life.'

'What do you want.'

'You. That's it. Like most women, I'm a fool about one man. No matter what you are, you are what I want. I'm willing to destroy my reputation and say that you were with me in Mahabalipuram — in a single room — but in exchange I want a wedding. Simple, Kamal. I want you to marry me.'

I stared at her. I tried to breathe. But her perfume overwhelmed me. I almost gagged.

'Make up your mind, Kamal. You think I won't hit back at you for the shameful way you've used me? Try it. Just crowd me. You'll see.'

YOU CAN JUST TAKE SO MUCH at a time, and no more. I felt nothing but fatigue.

It was late in the afternoon before Govinda Raju returned. A police vehicle stood outside all day. But nobody spoke to me. I suppose I could have walked out through the back door and kept walking. I do not know. I did not try it.

I prowled the house trying to guess what Sarita was going to do. She had let me know. I could marry her — or go to the gallows.

I walked into the room where I had killed Seema. I stared at myself in the mirror. I laughed aloud. You stupid, ignorant, son of a bitch. Oh, you were smart. Seema would go to Bombay, apply for a divorce, and then send a note, she was committing suicide. You would have to substantiate the fact of her death. But your status was in your favour, and of course bribes. It could have been done.

Sure there were angles. If I could not substantiate her death how would I expect to collect fifty lakhs of rupees?

And what if she had changed her will? But I had not hoped to collect through a will. We had a joint bank account. Many of her stocks and bonds were negotiable. I could get plenty, before I ever substantiated her death. No matter what the banks thought about my cleaning out our joint accounts, there was nothing they could do.

I wiped my hand across my eyes. They ached so terribly, but I knew I could not close them. If I slept I dreamed. Seema's rigid body would crowd me against a wall so that I must stay cramped and miserable till I woke up. Sure I had screamed.

That was what I had left of my big plans. Do not rush. Do not stampede. It will take a long time. Fifty lakhs is a big prize. And it will take time to do it right. But I was not moving slowly. I was rushing along. And time had lost meaning. I scrubbed my hands over my face.

'What's the matter?'

A sound burst out of my throat. I trembled all over and heeled around. Govinda Raju stood in the doorway. He was watching me. The worst part of it was I had no idea how long he had been standing there. Maybe he had been there all the time. Maybe he had been behind me watching all day long.

'You look beat, Counsellor?'

I stared at him. Waiting. I was not stepping into any trap. He was not even going to get the time of the day from me. Here was a fellow going to have to carry the ball all the way.

'I've been working, Counsellor. Been a busy day. Had a whole team of detectives working. Even being a lawyer as you are, I guess you've no idea how much you can accomplish in one day with a team of trained detectives working on one thing.'

I waited. My lips were parched. But I did not dampen them.

'For instance, I'll tell you something you didn't know. We matched up that picture of the man the Bombay Police were seeking. His name is Satya Pal. Mean anything to you, Counsellor?'

I shook my head. 'Ought to. Now that he's in the case, I've changed a lot of my ideas. You know who he is?'

'No.'

'You ought to keep up with crime more. Satya Pal is a hoodlum. Two-time loser. Served time for robbery. Just got out on parole a few months ago.'

'What does that mean to me?'

He smiled. A grim look boxed as it was between sagging nostrils and jutting jaw.

'It ought to mean a lot. His wife worked for you.'

'Wife?'

He shrugged.

'Why not? A girl has to work when her husband gets caught on a robbery and has to serve time.'

Robbery! It came back to me. Pushpa telling me about her friend, whose husband was up for parole, but needed help. Oh God. Pushpa was the friend. And Satya Pal was the husband. Small time hoodlum. Embezzlement.

'Only thing is that this Pushpa was afraid you might have heard of her husband. When she came here to Bangalore, she neglected to bring her married name with her. She took back her maiden name. Come to think of it, the old name wasn't much better.'

When they start, they do not leave you anything. 'Pushpa wasn't exactly an angel herself. She spent some time in the reformatory for girls.'

I shook my head. He stared at me and nodded, pleased

with himself. 'You didn't know much about her at all, did you? That's where they taught her typing and shorthand. Rehabilitation stuff. She had quite a story. Seems she'd been her uncle's mistress for a long time since she was about 14.'

I pressed my fist against my throat.

'It might never have come to light. But uncle killed his wife — Pushpa's aunt. It happened a long time ago. No reason you should have heard about any of it. But seems at the trial uncle broke down and admitted he'd been making love to his niece for a couple of years. They couldn't prove she had anything to do with the murder, or even knew anything about it. But the judge put her in the School for Girls so that she could be given training and rehabilitation. What a laugh! While she was in the reformatory she met Satya Pal's sister. And when he came to visit her, she met Satya Pal. Pretty picture, eh, Counsellor?'

I shook my head, thinking of all the lies I had once believed about Pushpa, and all the truths I was forced to believe now.

'If I'd known about Satya Pal from the first, I could have been easier on you, Mr Sharma.'

'What?'

'Sure. This punk being in this case changes everything. I got no more respect for you. I don't like you. I don't like men that can't live by moral laws — and you broke them with your wife. But I've changed my mind. I don't think you're guilty of murder. Satya Pal gives me the hook up I need.'

I stared at him, shaking my head.

He grinned, and I shivered at the humourless picture it made. 'Don't be dense Mr Sharma. Like I say, I don't like you. But now I think you were being taken. I don't know all the angles yet. But I will.'

'Taken?'

'Sure. This Pushpa and her husband were setting you up like a pigeon in a barrel. I almost have to laugh — the smart lawyer getting set up like a pigeon. Maybe they planned it that way. Pushpa goes to work for you. Then they fix up some kind of deal to get your wife out of the way — and I got bad news for you on that. Down at the Headquarters they all agree on one thing. Your wife is dead.'

'Why... why do they think so?'

'It stands to reason. They killed Mrs Sharma so they could let Pushpa pass as your wife up there in Bombay. They had sued for a divorce. Maybe the next step was to send a cheque with Mrs Sharma's forged signature to the bank and withdraw as much of her money as they could — and get away to some country where they have no extradition.' His laugh was hard. 'Maybe they'd go to Argentina, and then send you word that your wife was there.'

'But — you don't know my wife has been murdered.'

'We know this. We know Pushpa was posing as Mrs Sharma, and had sued you for divorce. And take that letter the woman next door got. I've already found out that your wife never wrote that letter. But we got some things that your little secretary had written — and the experts swear that the doll that wrote the letter to Mrs Sarkar also wrote all the specimens of handwriting we gathered from Pushpa's apartment. That's good enough for me. It would have been good enough for the public prosecutor, if she had lived.'

'But if what you say is true why did Satya Pal kill... his wife?'

'Still hurt to say it, Counsellor? I don't know yet. But the CID is looking for Satya Pal. When we get him we'll find out what he was thinking. We'll pull that baby's thoughts out of him with a cold pair of tweezers. Maybe they fought. Maybe Pushpa caught the clever bug from working with you. Maybe she was trying to double-cross Satya Pal. But the thing is, we got him in a plot to kill your wife — maybe even to kill you after you had collected your wife's money. We're looking for Satya Pal. We'll find him.'

'But — you still don't know that he killed her.'

'Who else? He was living across the corridor from her. All the liftmen and the bellboys of the hotel were gossiping about the time they spent together. After she was killed — and before she was found — he disappeared.'

'But you told me that I might have —'

'Don't you have enough troubles, Mr Sharma? Without taking on my worries. You told me that Sarita Shah would alibi you for the weekend.'

'You haven't talked to her yet?'

'I told you. I've been busy. Digging into the pretty past of your secretary. I'll get around to her. Right now, she's not what's troubling me. What I'm worried about right now is your wife. What we want to know is what happened to her after you quarrelled and you came back home alone.'

'I don't know.'

'Sure. And you haven't cared. You got the scent of this Sarita Shah. And all the time a hoodlum and his woman are setting you up either for murder or extortion. All the time they have followed you — Satya Pal must have — took over with Seema after you two fought and you came home. Somewhere he has killed her and hidden her body. That's got to be the answer. And now we're going to find out for sure and wrap this case up.'

'But how, if you can't find her?'

'That's it. We're going to find her. We're going to send a

description of her on the wire to every police department in the country. When a crime happens far enough away from here sometimes, we get only a whisper of it. Nothing to go on. But we're going all out on this. We're having pictures made of Seema Sharma — thousands of them. Somebody will remember her. And when that somebody comes forward, we can really slip the hooks to Satya Pal. Not for one murder, but two.'

I closed my eyes. I could not think of anything but Seema sprawled out on the front seat of that black Fiat, 2,000 kilometres away in Bihar. They had not been able to trace her back to Bangalore. But now they would have her picture. The Bihar Police and the CID must have taken pictures of her, when her body was found.

What if they caught Satya Pal. What if they got him to admit killing Pushpa. He would never admit killing Seema. But suppose Pushpa had told him all the things she and I had planned, suppose he knew the truth, and to save himself, he talked to the police. Why, it would be easy to make them believe I had killed Pushpa also.

That was what stopped me. Because when Sarita Shah got through telling Govinda Raju I had not been with her over the weekend, that would put another tint on the picture. Satya Pal did not even have to be smart. If he kept his mouth shut long enough, the stupidest policeman in the force would come up with the answer — I had killed Pushpa in a fit of jealousy when I found out she was working with Satya Pal.

I was tired. I had never been so tired in all my life. Not even the nightmare of driving 2,000 kilometres with a dead body on the back seat, without sleep, after a sleepless night.

I wanted to tell the truth. I was too tired to mess with it any more. All I had to do was say 'Govinda Raju, I killed

Seema.' That was all I had to do. It would be over then and I could rest. But I could not. Govinda Raju stood staring at me, but I was too tired to open my mouth.

WHEN I LOOKED UP AGAIN — Govinda Raju was gone. I did not even know for how long. I ran through the bedroom door. For a minute I completely lost my head. I wanted to yell at Govinda Raju. I did not want him to go out of this house and leave me here. What was the sense in waiting? It was just a matter of time, was it not?

'Govinda Raju?'

There was no answer. The sound of my voice struck the walls and battered to nothingness. I ran out on the verandah. The police vehicle had gone too.

But I did not feel any better. They had me. I could stay in this house, sleepless, waiting. Or I could yell till they came back for me. Everything I had wanted was gone! Everything I had tried to win was lost!

I looked around the house. I was alone. Perhaps for the very last time in whatever time was left to me I was alone. If I was going to do anything, this was the moment.

What could I do? Was there any sense in running? I was never going to be a judge in anybody's court. I was never going to have that fifty lakhs of rupees Seema had been hoarding. Pushpa was dead. I was no longer Kamalakar Sharma, Barrister-at-Law. I was Kamalakar Sharma, wanted for murder.

But at least I was still alive.

I looked at my watch. I could probably catch a plane north to Kashmir, east to Calcutta, or to New Delhi. Why not to Patna? Who would look for me up there? Who would think I was going to run in the direction they already wanted me?

My mouth twisted. Do not try to outsmart anybody Kamalakar. You tried that. The big smart lawyer, taking care of all the angles. Look where it got you.

Run. But do not try to be smart about it. Just be fast. If you hurry, you might make it.

How much time did I have? There was no way to know that. Maybe when Govinda Raju talked to Sarita and she denied being with me, he would come back and pick me up. Maybe they would not arrest me till after they had caught Satya Pal. In that I had a few hours, a few days. It was not much, but if I hurried, it might be enough.

I looked around. It was dark now. The darkness smoked through the house. If I ran, it would be an admission of guilt. But why split hair? Admit it, or have it proved? If you were in Brazil, it did not matter what they proved.

They might come looking for me. But it would take time, and time was all I wanted. Time to rest. Only now I could not rest. I had to get out of here.

I grabbed a cheque book, and let the door slam behind me. I threw open the garage door and got into my car. My hands shook so badly I dropped the ignition keys. I had to fumble on the floor for them.

I started the car. Switched on the lights. Something warned me they might be watching. And it was dark enough to get to the street without being seen if I cut the lights. Then I remembered the back-up lights would burn if I put the car in reverse. But it was a chance I had to take.

I reversed the car, moving slowly down the drive and out into the street.

I changed gears, and moved along the street. A car moved out in front of me from a side street. It pulled out and did not slow down though it was marked. At first I thought it was the police. I stared at the car. It was big. And of a dark shade. Not official.

I slammed on the brakes, pulled around and tried to go in front of it.

That was when I saw the car come the other way from the side street. It pulled up so I had to stop. The two black cars made a wedge and I was caught. Before I could reverse, two men were standing at the side of my car. My stomach turned.

'Just let it sit. Turn off that engine.'

I stared at them. Their eyes were dead in expressionless faces. I cut the motor. The silence pressed in.

'What do you want?'

'What's your name?' one of them said.

'You fellows can't do anything like this. There are people along this street.'

'You heard me fellow? I asked you a question. What's your name?'

The other opened the door. I caught at it. But he wrenched it free, stepped inside and leaned against it.

'Your name is Dinanath Kapur?'

I knew them then. They did not have to extend engraved visiting cards. I saw there were four others in the two black cars. All of them from the hot-car-ring, from the man whose name I had forced out of Sabapathy Naidu.

'You ever buy a car under that name? Black Fiat. Pay cash for it by telegram?'

'I don't know what you're talking about.'

He grabbed my shirt suddenly and dragged me from the car. I stumbled and hit the pavement on my knees. I tried to get up. But he twisted his fist, pressing me down.

'Look, Mr Kapur. Right in that car over there.'

They had left the rear door of one of those cars open. I saw Sabapathy Naidu sitting in the back seat. He looked battered. He stared at me. His eyes were cold.

I made a noise in my throat.

'Listen Mr Kapur. The boss sent us to talk to you. Seems you got him in a bad mess. Had the CID breathing all over him. He don't like that. Bad for business.'

The back of his hand across my face would have knocked me over. But he would not release me. 'Yeah, real bad for business. Boss said we were to impress on you. He don't like things that hurts his business.'

They dragged me up and fists worked me over, stomach and back. 'Boss pays a lot of money for protection. He likes things smooth. He don't like it when somebody makes trouble.'

It was as if my insides were being seared. Finally, when he released me I crumpled, my knees hitting the pavement.

'Get up, Mr Kapur.' He reached down, caught my tie and twisted it till I could not breathe. Slowly I got to my feet.

'That's better.'

The fists started again. The tie was twisted and the fists worked swiftly and professorially. I flailed out with my arms, no longer able to breathe.

'Stand still, Mr Kapur.'

Those hands went back and forth across my face. The tie twisted tighter. When they started using their knees, the agony was too terrible. I no longer felt it.

They released me and I hit the ground hard. I flopped around as I tried to get my breathing started, again.

Every time I moved, one of them kicked me, in the head or in the stomach. It did not seem to matter to them. I could not lie still, because I could not breathe again unless I moved. But finally I realised they were going to keep beating and kicking me as long as I moved.

I lay still, gasping for breath. They kicked me again. But they seemed to have gone far away. My head spun. My arm twisted. And again they kicked me. Then I was like slime on the street, without bones or muscles.

They lifted me, shoved me back under the steering wheel of my car. They started the engine and put it in gear. The car rolled slowly forward, going crazily down the street, till it bumped the kerb, rolled up on the parkway and came to a stop against a tree.

FINALLY, when I could breathe again, I sat up. The agony flushed through me and I almost passed out. I tried to start the car. I tried to drive. But I could not. I managed to open the door. I let myself fall to the parkway. At last I tried to stand. But when I did, the night wheeled round me and I knew I could not walk.

I took a step and fell flat on my face. I stared back through the dark street to my driveway. It seemed an impossible distance. I crawled over into the darkness and moved on my hands and knees all the way to my yard.

I got up then, staggered and fell. Got up, staggered and fell. Got up, staggered and fell, till I was back in the house.

Inside the door, I fell and lay there till I could breathe again. It hurt. But I could do it. At last I pulled myself up and started dragging myself along the wall to my bedroom.

Suddenly, a light from the front room struck me in the face. I was too tired to care. Too tired to react.

'Well, lover boy. Look at lover boy. Lover boy you look bad. You look like you caught your death of knuckles.'

I opened my eyes and stared at him. He was standing inside the front room door. Beyond him I saw the blinds were tightly drawn. He looked haggard, but he was in better shape than I was. His clothes looked mussed and sweated. His collar was still turned up about his neck. But I recognized Satya Pal. He was the man on the run. He looked it.

'What are you doing here?' Blood ran out of my mouth, when I spoke.

'Came to see you, lover.'

'You, you had any sense, you'd be out of this country. Police are looking for you.'

'Let them look. Exercise won't hurt them. Most policemen look like slops because they don't get enough exercise. So let them look. Just don't waste my time. I haven't got a lot of it.'

'They know you killed Pushpa.'

'Do they? You think it's going to do them much good?' He laughed. 'You think it's going to do you much good?'

I did not answer him. I leaned against the wall, just feeling good because I could breathe again.

'Look, lover boy. You don't look like you can take very much more. And I'm a man who knows tricks that'll hurt you in new places. I got no temper. All I want from you is money. As much of Seema Sharma's money as you can get your hands on.'

'Right now?' I smiled at him. 'None of it.'

'Okay. So tomorrow you get it. I'm out of the country and you don't see me any more.'

'What makes you think I can get Seema's money?'

'What makes you think I'm going to argue with you about it? Seema won't care. I know that. Out there in Bihar, she's past caring.'

I stared at him. Pushpa had told him everything. He read my thoughts.

'That's right. She didn't hold back on her Satya. No more than you will when you know the things I can do to your nerves. She even told me you've a joint bank account with Seema.'

'All I'd have to do is draw a big amount with Seema missing and I'd have the police all over me.'

'Oh, stop dreaming, lover. It's just a matter of time till you've got them on you anyhow. So look at it the smart way. Money isn't going to do you any good. But it'll help me get out of the country. Ordinarily, I'd be greedy. I'd take it all. But my little trouble with Pushpa changes that. And I'll settle for enough to get me beyond the reach of these policemen. Now stop stalling. You want trouble, just stall. That's what our girl Pushpa did. Tried to stall me.'

He tried to laugh. But his face worked with something that was not laughter. His voice remained taut. 'I wanted her to come back down here and put the big squeeze on you and we'd clear out. But she wouldn't do it. Want to hear something funny, lover? She fell for you. Man, the way she fell for you!'

It was self torture. But he could not stop. 'Man you should have seen that little scene when she told me she wouldn't put the arm on you for all that loot.' He shook his head. 'She changed after she went to work for you. Got too classy for Satya — tried to deal me out. But I'd never have killed her — not till she pushed me too hard.'

I stared at him for a long time. I said slowly, 'I'm no good Satya. Maybe I never knew how rotten I was till you walked in here. I can look at you and see what I am. I don't like it. I fooled myself with a lot of fine talk, but all the time I was slimy — like you. But this is it. You killed

Pushpa. That's too bad. Because I'm going to fix you. For Pushpa.'

He stood there, watching me. I managed to straighten up. I walked the ten long paces to the telephone. I was sweating.

'Run, Satya.' I said. 'I'm calling the police. I'm too beat to run. Too tired to fight any more. You're right. I'm not going to get away. But you aren't either.'

He sprang through the doorway and lunged at me. His fist knocked the receiver from my hand. He slapped the telephone off the table.

I grabbed at him. His right hand was in his pocket. I caught at it. I covered a gun. I tried to hold it pushed against the bottom of the pocket. But I did not have strength enough. His left fist caught me beside the head and spun me round.

I closed my fingers on that gun hand, holding on. I stumbled around, falling away from him and clinging to that gun. I heard a sound like a muffled shot.

The impact in the small of my back sent me sprawling forward. It tore my grasp loose from Satya's pocket and knocked me off my feet. I struck against the wall and slid down it slowly.

I fell on my knees and tried to turn. But I could not. The movement made me dizzy. And I toppled on my side. Gradually, I saw the fuzzy outline of Satya standing staring down at me. He said something, but I did not hear what it was. There was this terrible pounding in my ears. I kept telling myself I had to get up. But I could not force my legs to move. Distantly I heard the front door slam.

I lay there cursing myself. Never able to do anything you vow. You were going to get away with murder and collect fifty lakhs of rupees. And you could not do that. You were going to stop Satya because he killed Pushpa.

I tried to force myself to my feet. But no message reached my legs at all. I could lie there feeling the tears well up in my eyes and spill down my cheeks.

Abruptly there were sounds like thunder from my front yard. But they were not thunder. They were too rapid. Too sharply defined. Too near for thunder. It was gunfire.

I tried to smile. Satya had run into trouble. That was sure.

I LAY WRITHING. Die? Me? I can tell you this. People die only when they do not want to die.

I saw the front door open. I had a strange view of it from the floor. I saw their feet first, and their legs. Then I saw it was the police. And they carried Satya's bullet-riddled body.

Govinda Raju said something to them. And they dropped Satya's body as if he were something they had killed in the woods.

Govinda Raju came along the hall. I watched his legs move, his feet. He bent down beside me. 'Sharma's been shot,' he said. 'In the spine, looks like. Better call a doctor.'

Sure, I thought, keep me alive. Pamper me. All the way to the gallows.

Three days later, Dr Jagannath gave me the diagnosis. 'The bullet splintered your spine, near the base,' he said. 'At that you were lucky.'

'Sure.'

'You're alive. You can't walk. You'll be confined to a wheel-chair or bed the rest of your life. But there are compensations. You're good for some things. Reading. Talking. It's just that you're never going to walk any more.'

Govinda Raju was beaming. He sat in the white hospital chair beside my bed. 'Like I told you, Mr Sharma. We cleaned it up. All the way up. We got a report Satya was headed this way. It didn't make sense but we put a stake out. I figured he was trying to take you for something and came here to do it.'

I did not say anything. In the days since Satya shot me, I had done some heavy thinking about him. And about Pushpa and me. Pushpa had whatever it is that drives the men who love her off their rocker. I know what she did to me. Maybe that is what she did to Satya. It must have driven him mad when he learned his wife had fallen in love with me, and was walking out on him. And then he had come up here, to Bangalore.

I thought about it. And it seemed to be that he had done to me just what he wanted to do. If he could have got money from me, he would have taken it, sure. But what was the most he could hope for, knowing the set-up with Seema's money? A few thousand rupees at the most. Not very much, compared to his life. But he had not been thinking about his life. He wanted to hit at the fellow who had taken Pushpa from him.

He had forgotten about escape. He had killed Pushpa in that raging jealousy. But that had not been enough. I was still alive. And he could not rest till he had evened the score.

It looked about even…

Govinda Raju said, 'What do you think about it?'

'About what?'

'Haven't you been listening to me?'

'Should I have been?'

'Listen, Mr Sharma, I knew you lawyers think us policemen are stupid. But I got news for you. If it hadn't been for all the work I done on this case, you'd be headed for the gallows right now.'

I stared at him, speechlessly.

'That's right,' he said, misunderstanding my look. 'Now Satya got killed trying to get away from your house. So he can't confess. But we've to build his story the way it has to be. But there are a lot of funny angles. And some people were hot to elect you as the killer.'

'But not you?'

'Not me. I figure you're stupid enough to chase women, but not stupid enough to murder. Now here's the catch. With Satya as the killer, there are too many unexplained angles. But I finally convinced them that he had planned some kind of extortion after he killed your wife —'

'Killed my wife?'

'Yeah. We cleared that one. Mrs Sharma was killed and left out in a Bihar wheat field. Now that's just the kind of thing Satya would pull. I'll say this for him. Part of it was clever. A Bihar number-plate, stolen from a car in Bombay. That checks, he was up there. A stolen car, gotten from his hoodlum friends. He had been in with them. The kind of it only another hoodlum would have. There was no way to tie that car down. I mean no way. The CID tried all its tests, road dirt, film, fingerprints, and nothing checked out. Your wife and the car seemed to belong nowhere. They even got desperate enough to test the water in the radiator.'

'What for?'

'Mineral deposits. They got nowhere. Then they were going to send pictures of Seema to all the regions. Maybe they'd hit. They'd failed every other way.'

'I see.'

Just when they were about to throw up their hands, they found out something. They were able to trace the car to a hot-car ring in Secunderabad. They questioned the owner of this ring. But he gave them hardly any clues. However, the police got a lead from one of the guys working there that Satya was a close friend of the owner. It adds up.'

'And you know Satya did it?'

'Nothing else adds up. Not to me. No matter what they say about you. I figured you were chasing the Shah woman. You did a lot of crazy things — but none of them added up to murder. Not quite.'

'Did Sarita say I was with her that weekend?'

'Well, now, that was a funny thing. First when I went to talk with her, she said you were not with her. I can tell you it looked bad.'

'But she changed her mind?'

His jaw jutted. 'I told you I'll get the truth, didn't I? I know how to handle women. First I found out what proved to me you didn't kill either your wife or Pusha. Then I went back and checked with Sarita. She changed her story. Seems she didn't want to compromise her reputation — her words. She didn't want it spread in the papers that she'd been at Mahabalipuram with you. But I told her she was sending you to the gallows unless she told the truth. I explained to her why I knew you hadn't killed your wife and then she broke down and told me you were with her from Saturday to Monday morning.

I should have felt better. I did not. I did not ask him what his final proof was that I was innocent. I was ripped up wanting to know. But I knew better than to ask.

Govinda Raju nodded. 'You could have saved yourself a lot of trouble, if you'd spoken up. I had to hear from your neighbour.'

'Manjari Sarkar?'

'Yes. Mrs Sarkar. That was one of the reasons she was sure that Seema had gone off to Bombay. She told Mrs Sarkar the last evening Mrs Sarkar saw her that she was going to fix her will before she left, and Mrs Sarkar said she never did it, never got to. You must have known. But you didn't tell us your wife had changed her will when you started running around with Sarita Shah.'

I closed my eyes. Sure. That was Seema. Afraid something might happen to her and I would get that fifty lakhs of rupees. It was right in her character. I could hear her telling Manjari Sarkar, that Shah woman would never get her hands on that money.

Govinda Raju said, 'You knew your wife had left her money to charity. So I knew you hadn't done it. You just didn't have a motive.'

SARITA SHAH CAME that night at seven. She brought flowers. Combined with her perfume, the odour became intolerable.

'I hope we don't have to wait too long, darling,' Sarita said in a voice like a dull knife edge.

'Wait, for what?'

'To be married, darling, I might get impatient.'

I tried to laugh. 'Would you change your story again?'

She shrugged. 'I might add to it. After all, I know so much more. I know that you said Seema was leaving you — on the same night she was telling everybody you were going on a second honeymoon. If I told all that darling, it would all start again. Only I don't think it would end quite the same.'

'Why do you want me?' In my mind I was wailing in

despair. 'You know all about me. You know what I am. You must know that Seema's money will go to charity and there's no way I can stop it. Look what's left of me.'

She smiled, leaning forward. My nostrils distended.

'Oh, you're not so bad. I spoke to Dr Jagannath, darling. Before I changed my story to Inspector Govinda Raju. I found out that you are fine. You'll be in bed, but I can't ask for anything more. That's where I like you best. I'll always know where you are. You won't be out prowling around. And as for money — we don't need Seema's, darling. I don't have her fortune. But the settlement you got for me from Jay will keep us quite adequately. After all, darling, we don't need much. We'll have each other.'

I tried to tell myself I would get used to it. But a week after Sarita and I were married, I felt the way I had the night the hoodlums beat the breath out of me. I could not live without some fresh air. There was nothing but the cloying perfume, no matter what I did in Sarita's house. It was everywhere.

I wheeled myself into the bathroom. The scent was more potent in here. But I was not going to be long.

I pulled myself up and got a packet of razor blades. I was hacking at my wrists when Sarita ran in and knocked them from my hands. I lay my head back, gasping for fresh air.

'It's all right, darling.' She wheeled me back into that frilly bedroom. The curtains, the pictures, everything feminine and dainty and scented.

'I know you feel lost and cheated. You think your life is over just because you can't get around and walk. You don't need to. We're together, darling. For always. I'll be near you. Always. I'll take care of you. Always. Come, darling, let me love you. You'll be so glad you're alive.'

That day she bought an electric razor. Since then she has watched me closely. She pretends she is not watching me, but never lets me out of her sight. She never lets me get away far enough so I can get a deep breath of fresh air.

All I live for now is the moment when she will get careless. She will forget to watch me. And I will find some way to kill myself. There has got to be a way. I cannot breathe any more in this bedroom. And she will not let me out of it alone.

I think about Satya Pal. And I know he was lucky. He paid for his crimes fast. He got it over with. But me? I am paying bit by bit. Everyday I wake up and pay a little more. Only I go on paying. And never end. Never cease for a moment.

She comes upon me and slips her arms about me. And she never gets tired. There is no way to escape her. She keeps at me. And nothing discourages her. She invents a hundred new ways to excite me — as she calls it.

One thing. I can sleep. I cannot breathe, but I can sleep. Sometimes I dream about Seema. But it is not so bad. I no longer wake up screaming when I dream about Seema. No. Not when I dream about Seema. I do not wake up screaming. Not me. It is very much different now. Deep inside my mind where Sarita cannot hear me, I scream myself to sleep. Each night. Every night. This is the price I pay for the Perfect Murder.

ABOUT THE AUTHOR

Born in a well-known family of Brahmin priests in Bangalore, Shakuntala Devi received her early lessons in mathematics from her grandfather. By the age of five, she was recognised as a child prodigy and an expert in complex mental arithmetic. A year later she demonstrated her talents to a large assembly of students and professors at the University of Mysore.

Hailed as an authentic heroine of our times her feats are recorded in the *Guinness Book of World Records*. She has made international headlines for out-performing and out-computing the most sophisticated computers in the world.

In this, her first book, she turns her attention to study the highly complex mental equations of a human mind gripped by greed, lust and selfishness.

ALSO BY SHAKUNTALA DEVI

Astrology for You

Awaken the Genius in Your Child

Book of Numbers

Figuring: The Joy of Numbers

In the Wonderland of Numbers

Mathability: Awaken the Math Genius in Your Child

More Puzzles to Puzzle You

Puzzles to Puzzle You

Super Memory